ISBN: 978-1-945325-85-4

Published by Ornamental Publishing LLC

HARRY MOORE

PEN NAME OF AUTHORS
STEPHEN ANGUS DOUGLAS COX (1863-1944)
AND
CECIL BURLEIGH (1851-1921)

On January 4, 1901, an explosive new action-adventure book series, *The Liberty Boys of '76*, first hit newsstands. This thrilling series didn't just entertain young readers, it also taught them about real historic events and figures from the American Revolutionary War of 1776.

Penning the series were S. A. D. Cox, a former newspaper editor from Illinois, and Cecil Burleigh, an adventure fiction writer from New York.

In the pages of *The Liberty Boys of '76*, Cox and Burleigh transported kids back in time to witness historic battles, meet legendary patriot heroes like Paul Revere and George Washington, and experience the fight for independence from the British Empire alongside the brave, young Captain Dick Slater.

Ever dedicated to historical accuracy, the authors drew heavily from Benson John Lossing's acclaimed 1851 work, *The Pictorial Field-Book of the Revolution*, to ensure their details were correct. They were also well-known visitors at nearby libraries and bookstores, always researching new historical information.

Stephen Angus Douglas Cox wrote *Liberty Boys* adventures for many years, eventually moving on to Humboldt, Kansas, where he published *The Humboldt Daily Herald* newspaper until his death in 1944.

As for Cecil Burleigh, he authored countless adventure stories in addition to *Liberty Boys* over a very long writing career spanning 35 years. He eventually retired to the quiet life in West Nyack, New York, where he died peacefully in 1921.

With this new edition of Cox and Burleigh's most celebrated adventure series, we hope a new generation of young Americans can learn the importance and cost of freedom, patriotism, and American history, just like their great-grandparents did when they were little.

— The Editors

HISTORICAL NOTE

It is early December, 1776. Chased by the much larger British invasion forces, George Washington and his armies have retreated from New York, retreated from New Jersey, and now are taking refuge on the southern side of the Delaware River in Pennsylvania.

The only thing that can save George Washington now is General Charles Lee and his thousands of Patriot soldiers. But General Lee has refused to come and help, despite many calls for his assistance.

Is the cause of American liberty lost?

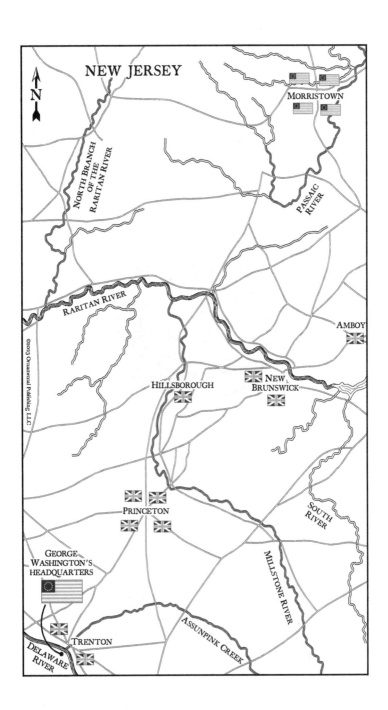

NEW JERSEY

N

MORRISTOWN

NORTH BRANCH OF THE RARITAN RIVER

PASSAIC RIVER

RARITAN RIVER

AMBOY

©2023 Ornamental Publishing LLC

NEW BRUNSWICK

HILLSBOROUGH

SOUTH RIVER

PRINCETON

MILLSTONE RIVER

GEORGE WASHINGTON'S HEADQUARTERS

ASSUNPINK CREEK

TRENTON

DELAWARE RIVER

PROCLAIM LIBERTY
THROUGHOUT THE LAND

THE LIBERTY BOYS OF '76

BOOK 7

HARRY O. MOORE

The Liberty Boys In Demand

OR

THE CHAMPION SPIES OF THE REVOLUTION

BY HARRY O. MOORE

CHAPTER I.

TWO LIBERTY BOYS.

"This is cold work, Dick."

"So it is, Bob."

"I almost wish we might run across some redcoats, so as to enable us to get our blood circulating."

"We will probably find some redcoats some time to-day. They are between us and the patriot army, you know, and we will have hard work to get past them without being seen."

"True."

It was a cold morning in the early part of December, 1776.

Two youths were riding along the road leading from

New Brunswick to Princeton, in New Jersey.

The youths were Dick Slater and Bob Estabrook, two patriots, and in addition to being members of a company of youths of their own age, known as the "Liberty Boys of '76," they were dispatch bearers high in favor with the commander-in-chief of the Continental Army.

The youths had been over to New York, and had borne dispatches to General Lee at North Castle, ordering him to bring his army of seven thousand men across the Hudson River into New Jersey, and join the army under Washington.

The commander-in-chief had sent several such orders, but General Lee, who aspired to the position of commander-in-chief in Washington's place, had refused to move his portion of the army, with the result that General Washington, with less than five thousand men, had been forced to retreat before the army of the British, under Cornwallis.

Had Lee moved his army when first ordered to do so, two weeks before, the commander-in-chief of the patriot army could have retreated at his leisure, and shown fight occasionally, thus holding the British in check, instead of having to flee at every approach of the redcoats, as had been the case.

Dick and Bob were very angry at General Lee.

They had borne several orders to him from the commander-in-chief, and they had a good understanding of the situation.

They had left New Brunswick only a mile or so behind them, and there had been informed of the state of affairs ahead of them by a patriot, and when they learned that the patriot army was simply running to keep out of the way of the British, their anger toward General Lee grew apace.

"Say, don't you know, Bob, I hate General Lee more and more, the more I think of him and his scandalous conduct!" said Dick.

"If he had done as he was ordered, and come over and joined General Washington, this retreat across New Jersey would not have been a hurried flight, as is now the case. I think that man ought to be court-martialed!"

"That's what I think, Dick. Just think! That man, back there, said that hundreds of our brave boys had scarcely any foot-covering at all, and that many of them left their footprints in blood on the frozen ground! Just think of that, Dick!"

"I have thought of it, Bob! I am thinking of it, and the more I think of it the more I believe I should be tempted to shoot General Lee if he were standing before me now!"

"And it would serve him right!"

The youths rode onward, and everywhere along the route they saw ample evidence that armies had passed this way.

Fences were torn down, barnyards were barren of any sign of animal life, the chickens, ducks, geese and pigs having gone to assuage the pangs of hunger in the breasts of patriots and redcoats alike.

They reached Princeton three hours later, and went to a tavern to get something to eat, and to get warm.

There were a number of men in the barroom of the tavern, and Dick and Bob were scrutinized rather closely by some of the more curious minded.

The youths, as they sat at the table in an adjoining room, could hear the conversation of the men in the barroom, and then soon learned that the topic of discussion was politics.

That nearly all of those in the room were Tories was evident, for the majority denounced General Washington and the patriots, and gave utterance to the hope that Lord Cornwallis would soon capture them.

"I tell you, Washington and all the rebels are as big cowards as they are traitors!" said one big, swaggering individual who had been very loud in his denunciations; "they are running from the British like scared rabbits before a hound, and they were never stand and make a fight. They haven't the courage!"

This was too much for Dick.

He had been listening to the talk with rising anger, and this was the straw too much.

He shoved his chair back from the table, leaped to his feet, strode into the barroom and confronted the big blusterer.

"So you are of the opinion that General Washington and all the 'rebels', as you call them, are cowards, do you?" Dick asked, in a quiet, self-contained, but menacing tone.

"That's what I said, young feller," was the reply.

The big man hardly knew what to think of the youth.

There was something in the clear gaze of the young eyes that abashed him, for he stepped back a pace looked slightly confused and taken aback.

"I heard you say it," said Dick, coldly; "that's the reason I came out here. I wish to prove to your satisfaction, and to the satisfaction of your friends here, that you are a liar!"

"W-what's that!" gasped the big man; "d'ye mean to say as how ye dare to call me a liar?"

"Why, certainly; and I am going to prove it, too. You said General Washington and all the 'rebels' were cowards and I am going to prove to you that at least one 'rebel' is not a coward, and if one is not, then there can be no doubt that there are hundreds, thousands who are not cowards.

Then Dick reached out quickly, and seizing the big nose between his fingers, he gave it a twist that elicited howl of pain from its owner.

"Down on your knees!" cried Dick, his voice grim and deadly now; "down, I say."

The youth gave another severe sidewise tweak of the nose as he spoke, and the big fellow dropped upon his knees with a promptness that was very satisfying to Dick.

The majority of the onlookers were in sympathy with the big man, however, and several made a move to attack Dick.

They stopped promptly, however, for Bob had followed his companion into the barroom, and as the men began to advance, he drew his pistols, extended them, an in a cool, calm voice, said:

"Stand back, gentlemen! This is to be a fair and square contest, man to man, and you shall not interfere. Just keep back, and attend to your own business. The big blowhard brought this trouble upon himself."

"I don't know that he is in any particular trouble," growled one of them, sullenly; "he will kill that whipper-snapper in a minute!"

"You think so?" with a quiet smile. "That is where you make your mistake. You fellows are making naught but errors this morning."

"You'll see!" sullenly.

"Now," said Dick, as the big man's knees touched the floor, "you will kindly repeat what I say. Any hesitation on your part will be followed by a tweak of the nose that will bring a howl from you. Ready? Now repeat:

"'General Washington is a brave and noble man, a thorough gentleman, and the greatest general of the world's history, and his men are all as brave as any men can be.'

"Repeat that, I say!"

The man hesitated.

Dick gave his nose a twist, and he yelled like a pig under a gate, with a redcoat holding said pig's hind legs.

"Now will you repeat it?" asked Dick, and the man gave a groaning assent.

The onlookers made another demonstration, but Bob held them back, and there was something in his eye which quelled and frightened them. There was a look that said "shoot!" as plainly as anything could have proclaimed it.

"Just you fellows go slow, and hold your horses!" Bob quietly. "If you make a break, and some of you are shot, it will be your fault and not mine."

"Go ahead!" ordered Dick. "'General Washington is a brave and noble man, a thorough gentleman, and the greatest general of the world's history, and his men are all as brave as any men can be!'"

The kneeling Tory repeated the words after Dick, in a stiff, halting manner; it was galling to his pride to have to do it so soon after having made the statement that the contrary was the case, but he had no choice in the matter. He was at the youth's mercy, as he feared his nose would twisted and pulled out of all resemblance if he refused.

"That was tolerably well done," said Dick, calmly. "You were a little bit lacking in enthusiasm, but we can understand that and make allowances; you would do better with another rehearsal or two."

"I'll have your life for this!" cried the man, fiercely.

"Oh, you will?" said Dick.

Then he gave the fellow's nose another twist, which brought howl of pain from its owner.

"Yes, I will! I'll shoot you as I would a dog!"

"Oh, pshaw!" said Dick, lightly; "I doubt if you could shoot dog at five paces, if you were to shoot at one. You are one of those blatant fellows who are all wind. You are not dangerous at all; your mouth is your worst weapon.

"I know this, or you would, otherwise, be in the army fighting for the side that you think in the right."

"I'll show you if I get a chance—"

"To shoot me in the back when I'm not looking, eh?"

"That is the only time that you would attempt such a thing. And to prove it I will let you up, so that you may have the opportunity which you claim you would like to have."

Dick let go of the man's nose, and stepping back a pace motioned for him to get up.

The fellow availed himself of the privilege quickly enough, but, as Dick had predicted, he did not attempt to draw a pistol and shoot the youth who had humiliated him before the eyes of his friends.

The man was a burly bully, and a coward at heart.

The treatment which the youth had given him had taught him a lesson.

He realized that his opponent, youth though he was, was dangerous, and he feared that if he attempted to draw a pistol and shoot him down said youth would prove to be quicker and better at the game than himself, and he would be the one to be shot down.

There was an air of conscious power in the very air and manner of the youth that daunted the bully.

So, taking counsel from his fears, he decided instantly that he would not risk trying to shoot the youth.

He thought of another way out of the trouble—a way that would let him out with credit to himself, as he thought. He was a big man, half again larger than the youth, and consequently, as he figured it, easily his superior in strength. He would attack the youth with Nature's weapons, and give him an unmerciful beating.

"I won't shoot you, on account of the fact that you are but a boy," he said; "and people would say I murdered a boy. I am going to have revenge on you, however, and I will tell you what I am going to do."

"What?" asked Dick, quietly.

"I am going to give you a good mauling with this!" and he held up a great fist, twice as large as Dick's.

"Oh, you think that will be safer, eh?" with a smile.

"No; but it will afford me greater satisfaction than if I were to kill you. Now, protect yourself if you can! I am going to give you a good mauling!"

"You look out for yourself," said Dick, quietly.

The big man rushed at Dick, and began striking out at him in the wildest and most reckless fashion imaginable. He evidently expected to land a blow soon that would knock his youthful antagonist senseless.

And, indeed, had one of the blows landed, it would have accomplished the purpose intended; but Dick took good care that none of the blows should land.

The youth was very light and quick on his feet, and he easily evaded the blows, until the big bully had winded himself by his exertions, and then he took advantage of his opportunity and knocked the fellow down with a well-directed blow between the eyes.

The fellow shook the house when he struck the floor, and he lay there, stretched out, blinking up at the ceiling.

He was dazed, and doubtless saw countless numbers of shooting stars.

"Get up," said Dick, coolly; "get up, and I will knock you down again, you big, bullying coward of a Tory!"

The fellow's friends could hardly contain themselves. They seemed on the point of rushing forward to attack Dick, but the pistols in the hands of Bob, backed up by the threatening look in the keen, cool eyes, were too much for them.

They did not dare to take the risk.

At this instant there came the clatter of horses' hoofs on the frozen ground, and one of the men who was near the door looked out, and cried:

"Here is a Company of the king's troopers! Now we will see whether or not these two young rebels can have everything their own way!"

CHAPTER II.

PURSUED BY REDCOATS.

Dick and Bob heard the sound of the hoofbeats as soon as any of the rest.

They had suspected that the riders were redcoats and enemies before the man made the announcement, and they had already decided what to do.

As the man uttered the words given above in a triumphant tone of voice, Dick said to Bob, in a low but decisive tone:

"Come, Bob; we will be getting out of here!"

As he spoke, Dick leaped out of the barroom into the dining room where they had just eaten their lunch.

Bob followed at his heels, pausing at the doorway just long enough to shake his pistols threateningly, warning the men not to follow.

Dick had a definite course mapped out in his mind.

When they had come to the tavern, three-quarters of an hour before, their horses had been taken to the stable, there to be fed and watered.

Dick knew the stable was fifty to seventy-five yards back from the rear of the tavern.

He knew there was a rear door opening from the kitchen out into the back yard, which was separated from the barnyard only by a low fence.

Dick led the way from the dining room into the kitchen, astonishing the cook not a little by their sudden intrusion.

There was no time for explanations, and no need of making any to the cook.

They hastened past him, opened the door and leaped out into the back yard.

They ran with all their might and leaped over the short fence into the barnyard, and raced to the stable at their best speed.

They knew they would have no time to spare.

The redcoats would be after them in a minute.

The Tories in the tavern would see to that.

The youths entered the stable, and singling out their horses at a glance, leaped forward and bridled them.

The saddles had not been removed, as the youths had told the stableman that they were going to stop only a short time.

Dick and Bob led the horses out of the stable, and as they did so there came excited yells from the direction the tavern.

They looked, and at that instant a score of redcoats came running around the tavern.

They waved their swords and brandished their pistols.

They were greatly excited over the prospect of capturing a couple of "rebels."

The inmates of the tavern had informed them of the presence of a couple of "rebels" on the place, and the redcoats had rushed out to effect their capture at once.

"There they are!" yelled the leader of the troop; "capture them alive, if possible; but if not, shoot them down!"

"We are in a tight place, old man!" said Bob.

"Follow me, and we will get out of it, Bob!" said Dick.

He leaped upon the back of Major, his magnificent charger.

Bob leaped upon the back of his horse.

"Lead on, Dick; I will follow!" he cried.

Dick gave a sharp word of command to Major, at the same time touching his flank with the spur, and the eager animal leaped into a run from almost the first step.

Dick dashed around the stable toward the rear, Bob close behind, and as they were disappearing the redcoats fired a volley.

A number of bullets whistled uncomfortably close, but none took effect in the persons of the youths or the bodies of the horses.

The redcoats uttered shouts of rage and excitement, and while some came running toward the stable, others ran back to mount their horses to give chase, in case those on foot failed to bring the daring fugitives down.

Behind the stable, at a distance of twenty-five yards was a fence, which divided the barnyard from a field of corn stalks.

This would be a good leap for trained steeple-chasers, but the youths did not hesitate.

They had perfect confidence in the ability of their horses to clear the obstruction.

They urged their horses forward to their best speed. The intelligent animals seemed to understand that the exigencies of the occasion demanded some unusual effort on their part, and they rose to the occasion and the necessity of the moment.

They showed no signs of balking, but putting all their strength into the effort, raced to within ten feet of the fence, and then rising into the air, cleared the fence without touching it, and raced onward across the field at their best speed.

"Brave boys! Glorious fellows!" cried Dick, and both patted the necks of their horses.

"Let the redcoats catch us now if they can!" cried Bob. The redcoats were evidently bent on catching them, sure, for they were now mounted—with the exception of those who had followed as far as the stable on foot—and were racing down the road toward where a pair of bars would permit of their entering the field.

This took them somewhat out of their way, however, and by the time they had passed through the gap, and started direct pursuit, Dick and Bob had got a start of nearly a quarter of a mile.

The youths soon found, to their satisfaction, that the redcoats could not gain on them.

"They can't catch us," said Bob, presently; "they haven't gained a foot."

"There are few better or speedier horses than ours, Bob," said Dick, in a tone of satisfaction.

"You are right, old man."

"Ah, yonder is another fence," said Dick, presently.

"There is a road there, too, Dick, isn't there?" asked Bob.

"Yes; how about it, Bob? Shall we take the fence, as we did the other, or dismount and throw it down."

"Let's leap the fence, Dick. The horses can do it easy enough, and it will give us a still greater lead, as the redcoats will have to stop and get off and tear the fence down."

"All right, Bob; I am—Great guns! Look yonder!"

Up the road, a quarter of a mile distant, in the direction Dick pointed, a band of horsemen were coming along at a sweeping gallop.

Their red coats proclaimed them to be British troopers.

Whether they were part of the band that had come to the tavern, or whether they were members of another party, did not matter particularly; they were enemies, just the same, and would work with the others to try and capture the two "rebels."

As yet they had not, strange to say, taken note of the race taking place over in the field, but suddenly the redcoats behind Dick and Bob saw the troopers coming down the road, and they set up a wild yell, which was calculated to attract the attention of their friends, and at the same time the yells were the expression of triumph.

Dick looked back.

The pursuers were still a quarter of a mile behind.

Then he looked at the band of troopers coming down the road.

There was evidence of excitement among them.

They had heard the shouts of their red coated friends.

They now saw the two youths and the pursuing troopers, and an understanding of the situation had come to them instantly.

They lashed their horses to increased speed.

It was their intention to head the fugitives off, and

capture them if they left the field and entered the road.

"I see what they are up to," said Dick, grimly; "but we will fool them yet! Follow me, Bob!"

Dick turned Major's head, and rode diagonally across toward the fence, Bob keeping close beside him.

Their new course would lead them to the fence at a point at least one hundred yards farther over toward the left.

"We will reach the road fifty yards in advance of that gang yonder," said Dick; "and if they do not bring us down at the first volley, I think we will be able to escape them."

"That's right," agreed Bob. "We won't give up till we have to, anyway."

This was characteristic of Dick and Bob.

Two braver youths never lived than they.

They had already, in the three months and a half that they had been in the ranks of the patriot army, performed many deeds of valor, both as soldiers in the ranks, on battlefields, and as spies in the strongholds and within the lines of the British.

They had had so much experience that already they were veterans.

No danger, however great, could daunt them now.

They had become accustomed to danger, and their only thought, when threatened, was of the quickest and easiest manner in which to escape. They never figured on being killed or captured.

Those who were pursuing the youths seemed to

understand what their plan was, and swerved aside and followed them, full tilt, while the redcoats coming down the road increased the speed of their horses.

"It'll be a close rub, Bob," said Dick; "but I think we will be able to get away, in spite of all they can do to prevent us."

When within twenty yards of the fence the youths urged their horses forward at their best speed.

Then, as in the former instance, when within ten feet of the fence they gave the horses the word, and the noble animals leaped into the air, and cleared the fence as smoothly as could be.

The next instant they were in the road, and racing down it like twin whirlwinds, with the band of redcoats fifty yards back.

The British troopers were yelling for the fugitives to stop, or they would fire, and, of course, the youths paid no attention to their commands.

Dick kept a sharp lookout behind him, however.

He knew the redcoats would fire a volley very soon.

Presently he saw the big dragoon pistols come out of the holsters, and he knew the moment was close at hand.

He watched closely.

Up came the arms of the troopers.

"Down, Bob!" he cried; "they are going to fire!"

As he spoke, he dropped forward upon Major's neck.

Bob dropped forward upon the neck of his horse.

As they did so, there came the crash of the exploding

pistols.

At the same instant, seemingly, they heard the whistle of the bullets.

Bob uttered a little cry.

"Are you wounded, Bob?" asked Dick, as he looked anxiously at his companion.

"Not seriously, Dick, I am sure," was the reply; "I felt something that seemed like a red-hot iron had been stuck against my side. I don't think it is more than a flesh wound."

"Let's even up the score, Bob!"

Dick drew a pistol.

Bob did the same.

Half turning in their saddles, they leveled the pistols and fired at the same instant.

The right arm of the leader of the redcoats fell to his side, broken, evidently, by one of the bullets, and his sword dropped to the ground under the feet of the horses with a clang.

A wild shout of anger went up from the redcoats.

The wounding of their leader angered them greatly.

They were doubly determined to capture the daring rebels now.

They would capture them or kill them, one or the other if it was possible for them to do so.

The body of redcoats that had chased the youths across the field had been forced to pause at the fence long enough for a half dozen of them to leap down and tear the fence away, as their horses refused to leap, and these fellows were now galloping along behind the other band of troopers.

Taken altogether, there were nearly a hundred of the redcoats.

There were altogether too many for the youths to engage in conflict, but their numbers did not make their horses' speed any greater, and the youths felt that their chances of escaping were very fair, providing no untoward accident occurred.

The youths soon reached the main road leading southward.

It was the road leading to Trenton.

They had learned, through inquiries made of the waiters at the tavern, that General Washington and the patriot army had been forced to retreat toward Trenton, the British having appeared before Princeton, and the youths were anxious to reach the patriot army, in whose ranks were the members of their company of "Liberty Boys," of which Dick was the commander.

So, knowing that the read led toward Trenton, they we glad to go in that direction, as the rapid pace at which they were traveling would take them to their destination very fast.

The trouble was that they were aware that the British army lay between them and the Continental Army, and if they allowed themselves to be chased forward in a straight line, they would be forced upon the main army, and be captured.

Dick communicated his fears on this score to Bob.

"We'll hope for the best, Dick," said Bob; "it is more than ten miles, and we will have plenty of time to drift away from the redcoats, and pull off to one side, and ride around the British Army."

"I hope so, Bob."

They were slowly but surely drawing away from their pursuers.

There was no doubt about that.

Their horses were better ones than those of the troopers.

The redcoats were determined and persistent in the pursuit of the fugitives, however. Doubtless they were insuring on forcing the youths forward onto the main army where they were sure to be captured.

The youths kept a sharp lookout ahead, as well as on their pursuers.

They did not wish to meet another band of the redcoats.

Onward they raced for perhaps four miles, and they were then at least half a mile in front of their pursuers.

They continued on another four miles or so, and had increased their lead to a mile. In fact, the redcoats could only be seen occasionally, as the country was hilly in places, and there was some timber.

"Don't you think we had better turn off into the first side road we come to, now, Dick?" asked Bob. "It can't be more than another mile or two to the Delaware, and we will run onto the redcoats somewhere between here and there."

"I guess you are right, Bob," was Dick's reply; "we will do as you say."

They did not come to any side road, however, and presently they entered a strip of timber.

When they emerged from the timber, they suddenly reined their horses up with a cry of surprise and discomfiture.

"The British Army!" gasped Bob.

Bob was right.

Upon a sort of plain before them were hundreds of tents and thousands of red-coated soldiers.

CHAPTER III.

A NEW FRIEND.

"Quick!" said Dick, in a low, earnest tone, "we must get away from here immediately!"

They turned their horses' heads back in the direction from which they had just come, and rode away.

They had been seen, however.

Shouts went up from the redcoats, and as the youths glanced back they saw the soldiers running hither and thither.

"They will pursue us," said Dick; "and if we go back in this direction far we will meet our other pursuers. We must take to the timber, Bob."

"Yes; and let's do it at once, Dick."

They selected a point where the trees were large and not so close together, and where there was not much under-brush, and entering there, they rode onward through the timber as fast as they could go.

They rode at right angles with their former course, the direction they were now going taking them up the river, and almost parallel with it.

"This is slower than when we were out in the open road, but I like it better in one respect," said Bob, presently.

"And that?" from Dick.

"It is much warmer here in the timber, where the wind can't strike us."

"True enough," agreed Dick; "it was rather cold work, racing along the road out in the open, wasn't it?"

"It certainly was! I was chilled through and through, but I'm beginning to thaw out now."

"We are in such close quarters with the British that they will likely make it warm for us before we get through with this adventure."

"Likely you are right about that, Dick. Well, we'll make them exert themselves enough so that they will be warm, too, before they get us."

The youths rode onward steadily, and as fast as they could, for more than an hour. Then, at Dick's suggestion, they changed their course somewhat, and bore away toward the left.

If they kept on in this direction, they would, sooner or later, reach the Delaware River.

"I suppose there is no doubt but that our army is on the other side of the river," remarked Bob.

"No doubt at all regarding that, Bob. The British are so close to the river that the patriot army could not be between them and the river; so I am confident that the commander-in-chief succeeded in getting across the river."

The youths rode steadily onward for three-quarters of an hour, and then suddenly came out upon the bank of the Delaware.

"Well, here we are," remarked Bob, as they reined up their horses; "and now the question is, how are we going to get across the river?"

"That is the question, sure enough, Bob; and it is a serious one, too. I doubt if there is a boat within miles of this place strong enough to carry our horses across."

"That is where you are mistaken, my young friend!"

The voice came from behind the youths, and they half turned in their saddles and saw a man standing within ten feet of them.

He was a rough-looking fellow, dressed in the garb of a hunter or woodsman, and he was leaning on the muzzle of a long rifle which looked as if it had seen service.

"Who are you?" asked Dick, rather sharply, for he did not fancy being taken by surprise in this manner.

"A friend, else it would have gone hard with you young

gentlemen," was the calm reply.

"How do we know you are our friend?" asked Dick.

"We have never met before, and I don't think you have ever seen us before."

"You are right about that," was the calm reply; "but I am sure we are friends, just the same."

"That depends," said Dick, quietly dropping his hand till it rested on the butt of his pistol.

The man evidently saw and understood the movement, for a half-smile crossed his face; but he made no move to show that he was alarmed.

"Depends on what?" he asked, quietly.

"On whether you are a patriot or a Tory."

"If I should say I am a Tory?"

"Then I should say that you were mistaken when you said we were friends!"

The stranger's shrewd eyes twinkled.

"You are bold, young man, in thus stating your position," he said.

"Oh, I don't know," replied Dick; "if you are a Tory and an enemy, we are two to one, which should be odds sufficient to insure a victory over you if you should offer to fight."

"I am not sure of that," was the cool reply; "however, it will not, happily, come to that, for I am, like yourselves, a true patriot. Who are you, and where are you from?"

Dick eyed the man searchingly, and somewhat suspiciously.

He was not fully convinced the fellow was what he claimed to be, and was not disposed to open up and give him information which might get to the British.

"It doesn't matter who we are or where we came from," replied Dick. "I won't dispute you when you say you are a patriot, but I must refuse to give any information to a stranger."

The stranger laughed.

He looked the youths over with renewed interest.

There was a look of admiration on his face, as he said, quietly:

"You are wise beyond your years; however, I think I know you."

"Indeed?"

"Yes; you are Dick Slater and Bob Estabrook, patriot spies, and members of a company of 'Liberty Boys,' now with the patriot army on the other side of the river."

The faces of the youths were impassive.

They were surprised at the knowledge which this stranger seemed to possess, but they had learned to conceal their thoughts and feelings under a mask of impassiveness, and they would not let him see that they were surprised.

"I will neither acknowledge nor deny," said Dick, quietly; "but who are you?"

"Who am I?"

"Yes."

"One who, he is glad to say, has rendered some little

service to the Cause of Liberty. My name is Joe Saunders and I was present and did what I could to help in getting the patriot army across the river yesterday."

"Very well; we will take your word for it," said Dick quietly; "and now, I am going to ask you if you can help us to get across the river?"

"1 can," was the prompt reply.

"And will you?"

"I will."

"Good! Let us hasten, then! We were chased all the way from Princeton by a body of British troopers, and doubt not they followed us through the timber. They are liable to come upon us here at any moment."

"Come with me," said the man.

He shouldered his rifle, and set off up the bank of the river at a swinging pace that tried the walking powers of the horses considerably.

Saunders kept up the pace for fifteen minutes, at least and then he turned to the right, and led the youths deeper into the forest.

At this particular point, there was so much underbrush and it was so thick, that, even though it was winter time it was impossible to see farther than twenty to thirty yards in advance.

Five minutes of this, and they emerged into a lit clearing, in the centre of which was a log cabin of fine size.

At one end was a sort of shed attachment, and Saunders told the youths to tie their horses in the shed.

"Take off their bridles and saddles," he said; "we will not leave here until after dark."

"Why not?" asked Dick.

"For the reason that if we were to cross the river in daylight some prowling band of redcoats would see us, and then when I came back to this side again I would be captured and the boat would fall into the hands of the enemy."

"You have a boat, then?" asked Bob.

"Yes—a flatboat large enough to carry your horses to safety."

"Good!" cried Dick; "well, we are needing rest, anyway, Bob; we have been in the saddle almost continuously about three days."

"So we have, Dick; well, I'm willing to rest here, and take it easy till dark."

The youths unbridled and unsaddled the horses, brushed them, and then the man brought a few ears of corn and some oats, and fed the animals, after which he led the way into the cabin.

At one end of the single large room of which the cabin consisted was a large fireplace, in which a cheerful fire was burning.

"Ah! that looks cheerful, eh, Dick?" remarked Bob, seating himself before the fire and holding his hands out toward the cheerful blaze.

"Yes, indeed, Bob."

"Are you hungry?" asked Saunders, as he threw another

log on the fire.

"Not very," replied Dick; "we ate at Princeton."

"I will cook you a bite, if you say so."

"No; we will wait till supper time," said Dick; "we will have a good appetite by that time."

"That's right," agreed Bob; "we can wait, and will be the better for it, besides saving you the extra work."

"It would not matter about the extra work; I would be glad to do it if you are hungry."

"No; we'll wait till supper time," said Dick.

The three sat there and talked for an hour or more.

It was now the middle of the afternoon.

"How came you to know the names of Dick Slater and Bob Estabrook?" asked Dick, presently.

"The commander-in-chief gave me your names and descriptions," was the reply. "He said you would be along this way, sooner or later, and he asked me to be on the lookout for you, as he wished you to be able to get across the river quickly, so as to hear your report."

Dick saw the man knew them, and his suspicions were allayed now, so he made no further effort to deny the identity of himself and Bob.

"I am glad we ran across you," he said, quietly; "I don't know how we should have gotten across the river otherwise."

"That is what is puzzling the British—how to get across the river," smiled Saunders. "General Washington secured all the boats for miles up and down the river, and he has them safe on the other side, so the redcoats will either have to swim across or wait till the river freezes over."

"I hope it won't freeze over this winter, then," said Bob. "I don't think they will try to swim across."

"Hardly," smiled Saunders. "They are not so eager as that to get at the patriots, even though outnumbering them three to one."

"That's right," agreed Bob; "and if General Lee, with his seven thousand men, had come across the Hudson River, and joined Washington's army, the redcoats would not have chased the patriot army so far and so fiercely."

"That is where you have been, isn't it?—up to where Lee is?" asked Saunders.

"Yes," replied Dick. "We were the bearers of orders to Lee, three different times, to bring his army across and join the army under the commander-in-chief."

"And he refused to move his army, did he?"

"Yes."

"The scoundrel!"

Saunders' eyes flashed, and his great hands clenched and unclenched.

It was evident that he was angry.

He held up his great right hand.

"If that traitorous Lee was here," he said, grimly, "do you know what I would do?"

"What?" asked Bob.

"I would take him by the throat with that hand, and end the life of a coward and traitor!"

"He would deserve it," declared Dick. "He has caused the commander-in-chief more trouble than the British have caused him."

"There is no doubt of that," said Bob.

"It is unfortunate that such men get into such high places," said Saunders.

"So it is," agreed Dick.

At last darkness began settling over all, and Saunders began cooking supper.

The supper consisted of venison, bread and coffee, and the three did full justice to the meal, as all were hungry.

"We will wait an hour or so yet before starting," said Saunders, when supper was over; "we don't want to start across the river until it is as dark as it will be to-night." So they waited another hour, and then they left the cabin, Saunders having placed a couple of logs on the fire.

It was snowing when they stepped out of doors.

Already a coat of white two inches thick was over all.

"I am sorry for this," said Saunders; "it makes the night so much lighter."

"True," agreed Dick; "still, there is not much danger that there are redcoats about, is there?"

"We never know, my boy."

Dick and Bob bridled and saddled their horses, and led them out of the shed.

"Now which way?" asked Dick.

"Follow me," said Saunders, and he led the way out of the clearing.

Entering the timber, they proceeded onward a distance of perhaps a hundred yards, and then they came to a little creek.

Saunders turned here, and led the way along the creek, the youths following, leading their horses.

When they had gone perhaps a third of a mile, they came to the bank of the Delaware.

At the point where the little creek emptied into the river the creek's mouth widened till it was thirty or forty feet wide, and overhanging bushes almost hid the water from view.

Underneath the bushes and vines was a flatboat ten feet wide and twenty feet long.

"Here we are," said Saunders; "we will soon be across the river now."

At this instant voices were heard a short distance away, in the timber.

"Sh!" cautioned Saunders; "lead the horses down the bank, and onto the boat; make as little noise as possible!"

The youths obeyed, and they did not experience much difficulty, as their horses were unusually intelligent animals, and seemed to appreciate the fact that silence was necessary to the safety of their masters.

As soon as the youths had got aboard the boat with the horses Saunders came aboard, and all stood and listened in silence to the voices, which seemed to be coming nearer.

CHAPTER IV.

WITH THE COMMANDER-IN-CHIEF.

"Do you suppose they are redcoats?" asked Bob, in a whisper.

"Very likely they are," replied Saunders, coolly.

"Redcoats or Tories," said Dick.

"Have your weapons in your hand," said Saunders; "we'll give them a warm reception if they come here and discover us."

"We will that!" from Bob.

The youths drew their pistols.

"Why not start across the river at once?" asked Dick.

"They would be sure to hear or see us, or both," was the reply.

"True."

"If we have to do so, after we are discovered, we will move out into the river."

Dick recognized the wisdom of this course.

If they remained where they were, and kept quiet, they might escape detection, and could then take their time in getting across the river, but if they tried to go at once, they would attract attention to themselves.

It would be better to wait.

They waited and listened.

The voices came closer and closer.

As well as they could judge, there was a dozen or so in

the party.

"It's a foraging party of redcoats," whispered Saunders. Dick and Bob nodded.

The voices came nearer; the three in hiding could hear the footsteps of the members of the other party.

The bank of the creek was seven or eight feet in height, however, and they could see nothing of their enemies.

But neither could their enemies see them, and this was comforting.

Suddenly the three heard an exclamation given utterance to by one of the men in the other party.

"Hello! here's a creek!" the fellow cried; "how are we going to get across it?"

"Let's go down it a ways; maybe we will find a place where it is narrower," said another.

"No; let's go up the creek; it is more likely to become narrower up the stream than down it, you know," from still another.

"That's so; you're a philosopher, Chilton. Come on, everybody."

Saunders gave the shoulders of Dick and Bob a significant squeeze.

"We're all right now," he said; "we will wait a few minutes, and then start on our trip across the river."

"I'm glad they went the other way," said Bob, coolly; "I should have hated to have to kill some of the fellows."

"That would have been unpleasant," said Saunders; "but," he added, drily, "it would have been even more unpleasant to have been killed by them."

The voices of the redcoats grew fainter and fainter, as they moved away up the creek, and when the sound could no longer be heard, Saunders became active.

He brought a couple of paddles, and handed one to Dick.

"One of you hold the horses; the other can help me," he said.

Dick handed Bob Major's bridle rein, and going to the end of the flatboat, he aided Saunders to push the boat out into the river.

Then Saunders and Dick placed the paddles between two pegs at the sides of the boats, and began pulling slowly and steadily, and the unwieldy boat moved slowly but steadily out into, the river, and toward the other shore.

It was slow work, and the boat gradually was forced down stream, but the opposite shore was reached half an hour later, and a landing was effected without mishap.

"How are you going to get back alone with that awkward boat?" asked Dick.

"I have a small rowboat here," was the reply, "and I will tow the flatboat back."

"It will be a hard job, will it not?"

"Yes; but I have done it before. You need not worry about me."

"Well, we must not let you go until we have thanked you for what you have done for us!" said Dick, earnestly.

"Don't mention it. I am always ready to do anything that

I can to aid the Cause. It was my duty to help you to get across the river, so as to enable you to make your report to the commander-in-chief as promptly as possible."

"True, that is the way to look at it," agreed Dick; "well, good-by. I hope we may meet again."

"We will doubtless meet many times, my boy. If you happen to be in the neighborhood of my cabin, drop in and see me; and if you should need help, don't fail to call on me."

"I will not hesitate to do as you say," replied Dick.

Then Saunders shook hands with the boys, told them how to go to reach the encampment of the patriot army, and then he began making preparations to recross the river, while the youths mounted and rode away in the direction indicated by Saunders.

The distance, the man said, was about two miles, and it took the youths nearly an hour to traverse it, as they had to make their way through the timber, and were, moreover, unfamiliar with the country, and went some out of their way.

At last they were challenged, however, and the "Who comes there?" sounded very welcome to them.

"Friends!" replied Dick.

Then he and Bob rode forward, and it happened the sentinel was one of the members of Dick's company of "Liberty Boys."

"Glory! It's Dick and Bob!" the sentinel cried; "I thought your voice sounded familiar."

"We wish to be shown to the headquarters of the commander-in-chief at once, Sam," said Dick, and the sentinel called the officer of the guard, and turned the youths over to him.

They were conducted to the headquarters of the commander-in-chief.

This was a log house, and when the youths were ushered in the main room, where a cheerful log fire was burning, the commander-in-chief and several of his generals were there.

General Washington was so delighted when he saw who the new-comers were that he leaped to his feet and advanced and shook hands with Dick and Bob.

"You have dispatches from General Lee?" he exclaimed, eagerly. "Ah! I hope he has obeyed orders, and moved his army at last."

"Here is a communication which General Lee gave me to bring to you, your excellency," said Dick, and he drew a document from his pocket and handed it to the commander-in-chief.

General Washington opened the communication and read it.

"Lee and his army are on this side of the Hudson at last, General Greene," he said, his voice trembling slightly. Then he turned to Dick.

"Where was the army when you left it?" he asked.

"It was a couple of miles this side of the Hudson River, sir, and headed for Morristown. It moved so slowly that we decided to come on ahead, and General Lee then wrote the letter and gave it to us to bring to you."

The commander-in-chief read the letter again, and then looked at his companion officers.

"I am sorry to have to inform you that the army under Lee has dwindled to only a little more than half what it was when we left it at North Castle," he said; "General Lee says that he has only about four thousand men."

"That is bad," said General Greene.

The other officers said the same.

"Still, with four thousand added to our force of three thousand, we will be strong enough to strike the British a heavy blow, I am sure," the commander-in-chief added.

"Yes; seven thousand men ought to be a sufficient force to enable us to do something," agreed Greene.

"The trouble is that it will be a week or ten days before Lee and his army reach here," said Washington.

"True," said Greene; "but perhaps it would not be a bad idea to send messengers, urging haste on his part. That might bring him sooner."

General Greene understood Lee pretty well, and he was sure that unless the commander-in-chief kept at the man he would be in no hurry to reach his destination.

Washington turned to Dick and Bob.

"About how many miles a day did the army march while you were with it?" he asked.

"Six or seven miles a day, I should judge, your excellency," replied Dick.

The generals looked at each other.

"At that rate it will take him two weeks to reach here," said the commander-in-chief.

"Perhaps longer, if he should meet with obstacles of any kind," said Greene.

"I think I had better send messengers every day or two, urging him to move as rapidly as possible," said the commander-in-chief.

"I think so," agreed Greene, and the other officers nodded assent.

General Washington paced the floor for a few minutes, and there was a sober look on his face.

Presently he stopped and looked at Dick and Bob.

"Dick," he said, "Harper and Bird are away, across the river, and I have no one to send to Lee, unless you will return, and that seems like asking too much of you. You have just come in off a dangerous and fatiguing trip, and ought, by rights, to have two or three days of absolute rest."

"We want but three or four hours' rest, your excellency," said Dick, promptly. "Write your orders to General Lee, give us four hours' time, and we will be ready to start again."

"Thanks! Thanks!" said Washington; "but it seems like asking almost too much of you."

"The more we are in demand, the better pleased we will be, your excellency," said Dick, earnestly; "we would rather be at work doing something than sitting idly here doing nothing. We are glad our services are in demand."

"Well said," said Greene, approvingly.

"Very well," said the commander-in-chief. Then he pointed to a door opening into another room. "Go in there and lie down and go to sleep," he said; "you will be called at two o'clock, which will be early enough to start, and will give you time enough to get across the river and away from the vicinity of the British before daylight."

Dick and Bob saluted, and withdrew, entering the room indicated.

They found several cots in there, and throwing themselves down on two of them, they went to sleep.

It seemed to them, when they were awakened at two o'clock, as if they had not been asleep five minutes.

They were soon wide awake, however, and on re-entering the main room of the house were surprised to find Generals Washington and Greene still up.

They were sitting before the fire, conversing in low tones.

Many nights, during these troublous times, the commander-in-chief of the Continental Army slept not to exceed three hours during the night.

General Washington gave Dick a document, which the youth placed in his pocket.

"Deliver that to General Lee," he said; "and bring his answer back."

"Very well, your excellency," said Dick, and then, after listening to a few words of instruction, the youths saluted and withdrew.

They went at once and saddled and bridled their faithful horses, mounted, and rode away in the storm and darkness—for it was still snowing.

CHAPTER V.

THE MEETING IN THE ROAD.

THE youths rode through the timber, going in a northerly direction, nearly parallel with the river.

They continued on in this direction for a distance of about two miles; then they turned toward the right, and were soon on the bank of the river.

The youths looked about them, but seeing no signs of any boats, they rode along the bank, going northward.

Presently they were challenged.

They responded, and a minute later were talking with one of the sentinels on guard over the boats which Washington had captured, and which, if kept on this side of the river, would make it impossible for the British to cross until after the river froze over.

There was a log cabin a short distance back in the timber, and it was here that the guard had their quarters, two sentinels being on guard all the time, and changing every two hours.

Dick explained what he wanted, and showed an order

from the commander-in-chief to the officer of the guard, ordering him to take the youths and their horses across the river, and he quickly awoke the four soldiers, and detailed them for the work.

Ten minutes later the two youths, with their horses, were on their way across the river on a flatboat, the four soldiers rowing.

When the other shore was reached, the youths led their horses off the boat, bade the soldiers good-by, and, mounting, rode away through the forest.

The youths were not very familiar with this part of the country, but they knew their general course must be toward the north, and they went in that direction as nearly as they could.

They gradually bore away to the right, however, and an hour later they came to a road.

"Good!" said Bob; "I'm glad we have found a road at last. I was getting tired of riding at random through the timber."

"I think we were going in nearly the right direction, Bob," said Dick. "However, it will be safer to follow a road."

"And much more pleasant."

They followed the road, which presently led them out of the timber into the open country.

Here and there they passed a farm house, gloomy and silent in the darkness of the early morning.

It was still snowing, and the weather was not, of course,

disagreeably cold.

At last the sun came up, and the sight of it was cheering.

"I'm hungry, Dick," said Bob; "let's stop at the next house and order breakfast."

"Very well; if the people happen to be up."

"Oh, they'll be up; people are early risers in the country, you know."

The sun was half an hour high when the youths came to the next house.

A man was out in the barnyard milking a cow, and the youths addressed him.

"Can we get something to eat here, sir?" asked Dick.

"I reckon ye kin, ef ye hain't too partickler what ye hev er eat," was the reply.

"Oh, we are not very particular," said Dick; "and we should like to feed our horses, also."

"All right; lead 'em inter ther barnyard, an' we'll put 'em in the stable an' giv 'em a feed."

The youths obeyed, and as soon as the horses had been attended to, the three went to the house, the man being through milking.

The youths ate breakfast, and while the food was far from good, it would appease the pangs of hunger, and they were not disposed to grumble.

The farmer and his wife betrayed considerable interest in the two youths, and asked numerous questions, but did not receive answers that gave them much information.

At the same time, the youths asked a number of

innocent-appearing questions, and managed to learn a few things regarding the British which might prove of value. After breakfast the youths paid their score, mounted their horses, and rode onward.

They had gone perhaps five miles when they met a body of redcoats, a dozen in number, and they drew themselves across the road in such fashion as to bar the youths' progress.

"Halt!" cried the leader; "who are you, and where are you going?"

"We are a couple of farmer boys," replied Dick, coolly; "and we live down the road a ways."

"Where are you going?"

"Up the road a ways, to get a cow that our father bought of a neighbor."

The redcoats looked skeptical.

"Hum!" the leader said; "that may be true, and it may not."

"Oh, it's the truth," said Dick, calmly; "why should you doubt it?"

"Because you don't look like farmer boys; you look more like rebels!"

"Rebels?—what are they?" asked Dick, simulating ignorance.

"You know what rebels are as well as I do, and I believe you are rebels, too! Ah! I am sure of it! I see pistols in your belts, and farmer boys would not be wearing pistols."

"Why not?" Dick wanted to know.

"What would you want with them?"

"To shoot anyone with who might try to take our cow away from us. They do say the rebels, as you call them, are hungry enough to eat anything, and if some of them were to meet us when we were driving our cow home, they might try to take her away from us."

The redcoat looked at Dick searchingly, and then he suddenly made up his mind, evidently, that Dick was not speaking the truth, for he drew his sword, and cried:

"You are no more farmer boys than I am! You are rebels, and doubtless are spies! Surrender!"

The redcoats were unprepared for what followed.

As the leader of the band waved his sword and cried "surrender!" the youths dropped the bridle reins upon the necks of their horses, drew a pistol with each hand, spoke a word of command to the horses, at the same time touching them lightly in the flank with their spurs, and the horses dashed forward, straight toward the horsemen in the middle of the road.

"Out of the way, or you are dead men!" shouted Dick, and so fierce was his tone, and so fierce and determined-looking the faces of both youths, that the redcoats got out of the way in a hurry—all except the leader. He tried to make his horse stand its ground, and he struck at Dick with his sword.

The youth swayed over far enough so that the blade did not strike him, and then he fired one of his pistols. The shot was of the snap-shot variety, he not taking aim at all, but a bullet struck the officer's sword-arm and broke it, the sword dropping to the ground.

Then, with defiant shouts the youths plunged through the opening made for them, and went on up the road like whirlwinds.

CHAPTER VI.

THE BOYS AND THE FORAGERS.

FOR a few moments the redcoats stared after the youths in wide-eyed and open-mouthed amazement, then the leader, who was suffering considerable pain from his broken arm, shouted:

"After them! After them at once, and capture or kill the scoundrels! They are rebels! Capture them if possible; but if not, shoot them!"

Then the redcoats woke up, and started in pursuit of the daring youths.

They shouted for the fugitives to stop, but, of course, Dick and Bob paid no attention.

"I don't think they can catch us " said Dick, quietly.

"I am sure they can't, Dick," said Bob. Their horses don't look equal to the task."

Dick glanced back.

"Down, Bob!" he cried; "they are going to fire!"

The youths dropped forward upon the necks of their

horses just as there came the report of the pistols.

The distance was too great, however, and the bullets must have struck the ground before reaching the fugitives.

The youths rode onward at the lively rate of speed at which they had been going, and the redcoats thundered along in pursuit.

Dick glanced back frequently, and was well pleased to note that they were drawing away from their pursuers.

He so informed Bob, who glanced back and saw that it was the case.

"Oh, we're all right!" he said. "They'll never catch us."

The redcoats evidently came to the same conclusion, for after chasing the youths half an hour, and finding themselves nearly half a mile behind and losing ground rapidly, they gave up, and turned their horses' heads in the opposite direction, and started on the back track.

"They've given it up as a bad job, Dick," said Bob, who was the first to notice the action of their enemies. "They're going back."

"So they are," said Dick, after a glance behind; "well, we'll slow down a bit, and let our horses rest."

They did so.

At noon they ate dinner at a farmer's house, and then after an hour's rest, pushed forward.

They arrived at Morristown at about half-past four o'clock, and stopped there an hour to let their horses rest. The snow had melted and made the roads soft, and the going was very hard, making travel very slow and difficult.

They ate supper, as they intended to push on and try find the patriot army under Lee.

They didn't know whether they would succeed or not but they had a pretty good idea where the army would be and they thought they would be able to find it.

At half-past six they set out on their journey.

It was now dark, though not quite so dark as it would be later on.

The youths followed the road without difficulty, however.

The road ran across the open country, and through strips of timber alternately, and as they rode into the first strip of timber, a couple of miles from Morristown, two men suddenly leaped out in the road in front of them and seized the horses' bits.

"Dismount, or you are dead men!" the men cried fiercely.

The youths were taken by surprise, but they were not at all disposed to obey orders.

Instinctively, almost, both did the same thing at the same instant, viz., struck their horses in the flanks with the spurs which they wore at their heels.

The horses gave utterance to snorts of pain and surprise, and plunged suddenly forward, knocking the highwaymen down and trampling on them, causing them to give vent to yells of pain and curses of rage.

Then, at a word from their masters, the horses leapt forward, and went down the road at a goodly pace, leaving the would-be robbers—for they could hardly be anything else—lying on the ground.

The fellows shouted for Dick and Bob to stop, but the youths merely laughed.

Then there came the sound of a couple of pistol shots.

The foiled robbers had fired after their escaping prey.

The bullets went wild, however, and the youths gave utterance to a shout of defiance.

"A couple of highway robbers; eh, Dick?" remarked Bob, when they were beyond pistol-shot distance of the fellows.

"I judge so, Bob," replied Dick.

"I wonder if there are any more such in these woods?"

"Hard telling; I guess not, however."

"I hope not; they gave me a shock!" and Bob laughed as if it was amusing.

"Such things are calculated to startle one, I will admit," said Dick. "I was a bit taken aback myself."

"But they were worse off when the horses jumped on top of them!" and Bob laughed again.

"Yes; I guess we are even with them."

The youths rode onward.

They kept as sharp a lookout about them as was possible, for they did not wish to be taken by surprise a second time.

They were not interrupted again, however, and when they reached the open country they were not afraid of another attempt being made.

"Where do you think the army will be, Dick?" asked Bob, as they rode along.

"I've been thinking, Bob," was the reply. "I should think it had got as far as the Passaic River by this time; what do you think?"

"I should think so, Dick."

"And we must be within five or six miles of the Passaic, I should judge."

"I think so."

They rode onward, and half an hour later entered the fiber growing along the Passaic River.

Presently the youths saw a glare of light in front and little to one side.

They rode forward at increased speed.

"I wonder what it can be?" said Bob.

"We will soon know," from Dick.

A few moments later they came opposite a clearing in the timber.

A log house stood close to the road.

A smaller, shed-like building, probably a chicken house, was on fire, and was burning briskly. This was what caused the light the youths had seen.

In the yard near the burning building were a number of men who, the youths saw at a glance, were Continental Soldiers.

"It's a foraging party of our own men, Dick," said Bob.

"You are right, Bob; but why have they set the building on fire?"

"To keep warm by, I guess, Dick."

The youths had brought their horses to a stop, and were watching the scene with interest.

Near the soldiers stood a man, a woman and a girl, and they were protesting against the burning of the building, to no avail, as the soldiers merely laughed at the words of the three.

"You ought to be burned out of house and home, you scoundrelly old Tory!" the youths heard one of the soldiers say; "and for two cents we would do it, too."

This seemed to strike the others as being the proper treatment to accord the Tory, and they began clamoring for this to be done.

"Let's do it!"

"Let's burn the old Tory out of house and home!"

"It'll teach him a lesson!"

"So it will!"

"It'll serve him right!"

The soldiers had evidently gotten hold of some liquor somewhere, and were ripe for anything.

"The boys have had too much to drink, Bob," said Dick; "I'm afraid they'll set the house on fire unless we interfere."

"That's right," agreed Bob; "they will stop at nothing, the way they are feeling now."

At this instant one of the soldiers ran forward and seized a blazing clapboard which had fallen from the roof of the chicken house.

With the blazing board in his hand, he ran toward the house.

It was plainly his intention to set the house on fire.

"While we're about it, we might as well have a good, big bonfire!" he cried.

A cry of anger escaped the lips of the owner of the house, and screams of protest and fear from the lips of the woman and girl.

"Please don't burn the house!" cried the woman.

"Oh, please, good sir; please don't!" the girl cried.

But the soldiers only laughed, and the one with the firebrand was just in the act of kindling a fire with the clapboard, when it was kicked out of his hands, and he himself was hurled back several feet.

"What do you mean? You must not do that!" cried a stern voice.

It was Dick.

He had leaped from his horse, run forward, and interfered just in time.

"What do you mean? Who are you?" cried the soldier, angrily, and then he got a glimpse of Dick's face.

"Why, it's Dick Slater!" he exclaimed, the anger leaving his voice.

"And Bob Estabrook!" exclaimed another soldier, who had approached.

Bob had followed Dick, and was right behind him.

"Yes; it is Dick and Bob," said Dick, quietly; "and now, Tom, what is going on here, anyway? Why were you going to set fire to the house of these good people?"

Dick motioned toward the man, woman and girl, who were regarding himself and Bob with eager, grateful looks.

"They are not 'good people,' Dick," said the man addressed as Tom, with a sickly smile; "they are Tories."

"And do you think that because they are Tories it is right to burn their house and turn them out into the winter's cold, homeless, Tom?" asked Dick, severely. "I didn't think it of you!"

The man looked shame-faced.

"I was a bit too hasty, Dick; I admit that," he replied.

"I should have thought the burning of that building yonder would have satisfied you," went on Dick; "that was uncalled for, I should say."

"Well, it's a chicken house, Dick," was the reply, with a grin; "and, as we have all the chickens, they have no need of the building whatever."

"They will want to raise more chickens, Tom. And, now, I will just say that I hope that you will not use the torch in future foraging expeditions. It is too much like the tactics of the redcoats, Tom. The patriot soldiers should be above such things."

"I guess you are right," agreed the man.

The other soldiers now crowded around Dick and Bob, and asked them where they came from.

The youths were well known and well liked, and they easily had more influence over the soldiers than any other dozen men could have exerted.

"We are on our way back to the army," said Dick; "where is it, and how far from here?"

"It's just across the Passaic," was the reply, "and it is only about a mile from here. You follow the road."

"Are you on your way back to the army?" asked Dick. "Yes; we'll go back with you if you'll wait a few minutes. There may be a few things in the way of food that we have overlooked."

"Well, don't take everything the people have, Tom; they must not be left to starve."

"Neither must we be left to starve, Dick," with a grin. "Of course not; but you can distribute your attentions around, and take some from all, rather than all from some."

"Of course that would seem the fair way to do, Dick; but we could take all from all, and still not have enough to eat. There are a good many of us, you know."

"That's true, too; but don't take all until you have to do so."

The man, and his wife and daughter as well, now advanced and thanked Dick for saving their home from burning.

"I have simply done as I would wish someone to do if my mother's house was in danger of being burned by the redcoats," he said, simply. "You are more than welcome for all I have done."

Presently the soldiers were ready to go.

The chicken house was now a mass of burning logs,

having collapsed a few moments before, and with the chicken in their hands the soldiers filed out into the road, Dick and Bob following, after bidding the man and his wife and daughter good-night.

The youths mounted their horses and followed behind the soldiers, who were exceedingly jolly, and sang doggerel verses in which King George played comedy parts.

Fifteen minutes later they reached the encampment of the army.

It was in the timber, and just across the Passaic River.

The arrival of the soldiers with the chickens was hailed with joy by their hungry comrades, and soon the quarters occupied by the regiment to which the company belonged was a busy scene.

Dick and Bob selected as sheltered a spot as they could find, and tied their horses there, unsaddling and unbridling them, and they covered the faithful animals with a couple of horse blankets, which they belted on.

Then they made their way toward the headquarters of General Lee, which was in a large tent near the centre of the encampment.

They announced themselves to the sentinel on guard in front of the tent, and he called an orderly, who returned to the tent and announced the arrival of the youths with a message from the commander-in-chief.

"Show them in," the youths heard, in a voice which they recognized as belonging to General Lee, and the next moment they entered the tent and stood before him.

CHAPTER VII.

KEEPING THE ROAD HOT.

"AH! you are back again, I see?" half-sneered General Lee, as the youths saluted.

"Yes; back again," said Dick, coldly.

Then he produced the document given him by the commander-in-chief and handed it to Lee.

The general took it, and then said:

"You may retire."

The youths bowed, and quietly withdrew.

The youths made their way to the quarters of a company that contained as many personal friends as there were men in the company, and they were welcomed heartily.

The soldiers had many questions to ask regarding Washington, his army and the British.

The majority of the soldiers under Lee wished to move forward as rapidly as possible, and join Washington's division, but Lee was moving very slowly, only a few miles a day, and was killing time.

It seemed as if he did not wish to reach Washington at all.

Next morning the youths received a summons, immediately after breakfast, to report at General Lee's headquarters.

They did so, and the general handed Dick a letter.

"Take that to General Washington at once," he said,

curtly.

"Very well, sir," replied Dick.

Then he and Bob withdrew.

They bridled and saddled their horses, said good-by to their comrades, and rode away.

It was clear and cold on this morning.

The ground was frozen hard.

It was rough under the horses' feet, but was, on the whole, better going than it had been the day before, when the melting snow had made the ground soft and muddy.

"General Lee doesn't have much to say to us, nowadays, does he, old fellow?" remarked Bob.

Dick smiled grimly.

"No; and I'm glad of it," he said. "I would insult him if I were to exchange many words with him."

"That's right; that's about what I should do, too."

They rode onward, conversing on first one topic, then another, and keeping a sharp lookout, for they did not know but they might meet a wandering band of redcoats.

They reached Morristown at ten o'clock, and stopped half an hour to let the horses rest.

They sat in the main room of a tavern while waiting, and listened to the talk of the inmates.

Sentiment was about evenly divided, those in favor of King George and those in favor of freedom for the American colonists being about equal in number. All had been drinking, and as the fumes of the liquor mounted to their brains they became more excited, and louder in their disputes regarding the political questions of the day.

Dick and Bob sat at one side, and listened with considerable amusement.

The men were so earnest, and so evidently thought that their decision regarding the matter should settle it, that it could not but afford entertainment for the youths.

Presently one fellow, who had been particularly loud-mouthed in his denunciations of the "rebels" and in his eulogies of King George, turned to the youths.

"What do you say about it, young fellows?" he asked, abruptly. "You haven't stated which side of the fence you are on."

"We prefer not to have anything to say on the subject," said Dick, quietly; "there are enough talking without our adding our voices to the din."

"Oh, but that is no way to do; that is cowardly, don't you know. You certainly have views on the subject, and ought not to be afraid to state them."

Dick's eyes flashed, and his chin squared itself.

Bob, who was watching his friend, and knew him so well, believed that there was trouble ahead for the subject of the king who had taken it upon himself to try to force an expression of sentiment from the youths.

"He'll find out whether or not Dick is afraid to state his views!" Bob said to himself, and he smiled in his sleeve to think how surprised the fellow would presently be.

"Neither myself nor my friend are afraid to state our views," said Dick, coldly. "We simply do not care to do so, that is all."

"But you've got to do it!" cried the young man, who had drunk just enough liquor to make him meddlesome, bossy and obstinate. "You've got to state your views!"

"So we have to state our views, whether we wish to do so or not, eh?" inquired Dick.

A person of discernment would have taken alarm at the tone of the youth's voice and the look on his face. It was threatening in the extreme; but the man never noticed it at all. All he saw was that the youth was an innocent-looking, harmless-appearing young fellow, and he had no idea that he was at all dangerous.

And this was where he made his mistake.

"Yes; that's it, exactly. You've got to state your views, whether you want to or not," the man declared.

"Well," said Dick, looking the fellow squarely in the eyes, "if I must, I suppose I must. Listen:"

All those present in the room had become silent, to hear what the youth was going to say. Doubtless the adherents of the king and those of Washington were hoping to hear a declaration for their side.

"Go on!" growled the man.

"Well," said Dick, slowly and gravely, "my views are as follows:

"That you are an impertinent scoundrel, and that, like the King George whom you profess to love so well, you are a knave and a would-be bully!"

Those who had been arguing for the independence of

the American colonies leaped to their feet, and cried:

"Hurrah for the youngster!"

The others sat still, and stared at Dick in open-mouthed amazement, while the man addressed gave a gasp.

"What's that?" he cried; "do you dare to speak in such fashion to me? Why, I'll—I'll—"

The fellow paused and gasped and sputtered.

"You'll what?" asked Dick, quietly.

"I'll wring your neck for you, you insolent young hound!"

"Proceed to wring!" said Dick, coolly.

The fellow was puzzled by Dick's coolness.

He hesitated and stared at the youth in an undecided manner.

Like the majority of blowers and bullies, he was a coward at heart, and there was something about Dick that awed him in spite of himself; there was a peculiar, dangerous gleam in the youth's eyes that warned him that their owner was not to be trifled with.

The fellow's friends were not willing the matter should rest, however.

They began urging the man to attack Dick.

"Spank the youngster!" said one.

"Teach him a lesson!"

"He's too saucy altogether!"

"He insulted the king, God bless him!"

"Do you mean God bless me or the king, which?" asked Dick, coolly.

The man, thus urged, rose to his feet, and reached over to take hold of Dick's coat collar.

Perhaps he thought he would do as had been suggested, and spank the saucy youngster, but, if so, he soon found he had made a mistake.

Dick seized him by the wrist, gave him a shove, and upset him, chair and all, on the floor with a thump!

Cries of anger went up from the Tories present and shouts of approval and laughter from the patriots. These latter enjoyed the downfall of the Tory and the discomfiture of his friends.

The man hastily struggled to his feet.

He was very angry, and it was evident that he would do the youth an injury if he could.

As he regained his feet, Dick quietly arose to his feet and faced him.

Bob quietly arose to his feet also.

He was ready to back his friend in any manner necessary, and it was evident that if a fight started, it would become general.

The fellow who had been floored by Dick so neatly gave utterance to a muttered curse, and leaped toward Dick.

Out shot Dick's fist.

It took the fellow fairly between the eyes, and down he went with a thump.

With cries of anger, the fellow's friends rushed forward to attack Dick.

But the patriots who were present were not disposed

to allow this.

They seemed rather glad than otherwise to have a chance to engage their enemies, and they sprang forward and interposed themselves between the Tories and their intended victim.

The next instant a free-for-all fight was in progress.

Dick and Bob took part, along with the rest, and they did able and effective work, too. They struck out with such swiftness, force and precision as to floor a number of the Tories, and at the end of five minutes the loyalists were a badly whipped crowd.

They took to their heels and ran out of the tavern, leaving it to the victors, and the latter gave utterance to cheers.

They gave considerable credit to Dick and Bob, and wanted the youths to drink in celebration of the victory, but the youths declined.

"We never drink anything stronger than coffee," said Dick, and then he and Bob excused themselves, and left the tavern.

Mounting their horses, they rode away, followed by the cheers of the patriots who had fought with them against the Tories.

The youths waved their hats, and then rode away at a gallop.

"We seem to be able to find trouble no matter where we may be, Bob," said Dick, with a smile.

"That's right, old man; well, we were not to blame for that back there."

"No; that fellow started the trouble himself."

"And had cause to wish be had not done so, too, before he got through with it."

"Yes; I think he did," quietly.

The youths rode steadily onward till about one o'clock, when, coming to a rather decent-looking farmhouse, they rode up to the door.

Dick leaped down, and knocked on the door.

It was opened by a woman of about forty years of age.

Dick doffed his hat and bowed.

"What would be the chance to get food for my friend and myself and feed our horses here, lady?" he asked, courteously. "We will pay you well."

"I guess we can accommodate you," the woman said, pleasantly; "you will have to put up your horses and feed them yourselves, however, as my husband is away at Morristown."

"Very well; thank you," said Dick, and he and Bob led their horses to the stable, placed them in stalls, and fed them.

Then they returned to the house and entered.

The woman was cooking, while a girl of about sixteen years was setting the table.

The girl was pretty and intelligent looking, and it was evident that she was favorably impressed with the looks of the two youths.

Dick, whose shrewd eyes seldom missed seeing anything, saw that the girl had placed a clean white table cloth on the table, and some nice glassware, such as would not be used for every-day service in the family, and he realized that this was in honor of himself and Bob. He saw an amused look on the face of the woman, also, but Dick never let on.

There was not a bit of the flirt in his make-up.

When the meal was ready, the youths sat up to the table and ate heartily, for they were hungry.

During the meal the woman and the girl asked some questions, and the youths judged from the trend of the them that the two were patriotically inclined.

When they had eaten, the youths paid for the food, and for the feed for the horses, then, bidding the woman and girl good-by, and mounting their horses, they rode away.

It was about half-past three when they reached Princeton, but, as they had not been riding hard, they did not stop there, but rode right on through, and continued their journey.

They had gone about five miles farther, when they saw a man approaching them on horseback.

The man's overcoat was open in front, and his blazing red undercoat proclaimed him to be a Briton.

"He is an officer, Dick," said Bob; "let's take him prisoner!"

"I was thinking of that, Bob," said Dick: "he may be the bearer of important despatches, too, and if we capture him, and secure the despatches and take them to the commander-in-chief of the patriot army, we will add considerable to our reputation as successful spies."

"That's right, Dick; we will prove our right to be, as the boys in our regiment call us, the 'champion spies of the Revolution.'"

"True; well, we will capture him. Let's dismount and tie our horses. If he tries to get past us, we can easily stop him."

"Of course we can!"

The youths dismounted, tied their horses, and then as the British officer approached, they stepped out into the road in front of the horse, and extending their pistols full at the rider's head, Dick called out, sternly:

"Surrender, and dismount! You are our prisoner!"

CHAPTER VIII.

AN IMPORTANT CAPTURE.

THE British officer brought his horse to a stop instantly. His ruddy face grew pale.

"W-why, w-what does t-this m-mean?" he stammered.

"Business!" said Dick, grimly. "Get down off that horse!"

The redcoat hesitated.

He seemed not to wish to obey.

The boy spies had the British officer completely at their mercy, however.

They forced him to dismount and throw down his arms, after which they eagerly examined the important papers which Dick found on the man's person.

"Ha! Bob, these are very important papers!" said Dick, his eyes glowing; "they are plans for an attack upon the patriot army, and this fellow is evidently on his way to New York to get General Howe's approval of the plan. We must take these papers to the commander-in-chief."

"And we must take this man, too, Dick," said Bob.

"Certainly; we don't want the British to know he has been captured."

Dick placed the papers carefully in his pocket, and then he turned to the officer.

"I shall be forced to tie your hands, sir," he said. "Place them together, behind your back."

The Briton objected, and protested.

"Give me back the papers, and let me go free, boys," he said, "and I will give you a lot of gold, and see that you get still more from our commander-in-chief."

"You waste your breath!" said Dick, coldly; "we are not traitors. Place your hands together behind your back.

"And hurry about it!" said Bob.

The redcoat saw he could not influence the youths, and reluctantly did as ordered.

Dick took a stout cord off his saddle, and tied the man's hands together; then the youths helped the man to mount his horse.

This done, they untied their own horses, mounted, and

leading the horse of the redcoat between them, they rode down the road.

The Briton looked blue and downcast.

It was evident that he took his capture very much to heart.

Doubtless it was the fact that he had become the prisoner of a couple of boys that made it so hard for him.

He would be blamed for allowing himself to be captured by the youths.

There was no help for it now, however.

He would have to grin and bear it.

He did not seem to be grinning very much, though.

Onward rode the three, and Dick and Bob were in a very good humor, for they had made an important capture.

They tried to engage the redcoat in conversation, but he was silent and sullen.

He seemed to prefer to brood.

It was almost dark when they came to a stop in front of a farmhouse.

"We'll see if we can get something to eat here," said Dick.

Dick knocked on the door, and it was opened by rather an ill-favored man, who eyed the three curiously.

"Can you give us something to eat?" the youth asked; "we will pay you well for it."

"I wouldn't be giving it to you then, would I?" with a grin.

"I meant can you furnish us with something to eat?" said Dick, coldly.

The man looked at the British officer, and then nodded.

"Yes; I can furnish ye with somethin' to eat, I guess; that is to say, the old woman kin. Git off yer hosses an' come in."

"We wish feed for the horses, too."

"Oh, yes; waal, bring 'em to the stable," and the man stepped outside.

"In a minute," said Dick.

Then he and Bob assisted the redcoat to dismount.

"You go in the house with him, Bob," said Dick; "I'll go with this man to the stable, and see that the horses are attended to."

Bob took the Briton by the arm and led him into the house, while Dick and the farmer led the horses to the stable.

The horses were placed in stalls and given some feed, and then the two returned to the house.

Dick, who was sharp-eyed and shrewd, took note of the fact that the man was watching him furtively, and the youth came to the conclusion that the fellow would bear watching.

"He is probably a Tory," the youth mused; "and he may even try to effect the rescue of the redcoat. I'll keep my eye on him."

They entered the house, and found Bob and the officer seated in front of the fireplace. The redcoat's hands were still tied, and the woman of the house, a large, virago-like woman, seemed unable to keep her eyes off the redcoat.

She gave her husband a peculiar look, and then glanced at Dick and Bob, and the youths noticed it, and exchanged glances.

They were not likely to be taken by surprise by anything the man and woman might do.

Nothing was said, however. The two seemed satisfied for the present to take it out in looks.

The woman was busy cooking, and a few minutes later she announced that the meal was ready.

The table was in the middle of the floor, and Dick noticed that the woman had placed two chairs on the side next to the fireplace, and one on the other side.

"A very neat trick," thought Dick; "Bob and I with our backs to the man and woman would be easy to attack. I'll just change that."

Then Dick placed one of the two chairs on the farther side of the table, and placed the British officer in the chair with its back toward the fireplace.

Then, untying the officer's hands, the youths went around and took the two chairs facing the officer, and also facing the fireplace.

The man and woman of the house looked disappointed in spite of all they could do, and Dick smiled to himself.

"They were figuring on rescuing the redcoat," said Dick to himself; "well, I'm sorry, but we can't allow it. We will have to disappoint them."

"Let's see; what did you say your name is?" asked Dick of the officer.

"Warwick," was the reply; "Captain Charles Warwick."

"Ah, yes; well. Captain Warwick, go ahead and eat heartily; we have quite a jaunt ahead of us yet."

The Briton made no reply, but began eating.

The youths did likewise, for they were hungry, and all went smoothly for a few minutes.

Then the woman came around behind the youths, ostensibly to help them to some of the food, but the youths suspected she had another reason. When they saw the man of the house come walking back, with the evident intention of passing them, and getting behind them, they were sure of it, and were on their feet in an instant, with drawn pistols in their hands.

"Back!" cried Dick to the man; "just keep back there by the fireplace, my friend, and oblige us!"

Bob had turned upon the woman, who stood, with fingers working convulsively, her eyes shining with a fierce light.

"You will kindly keep back on the other side of the table, my good woman," said Bob. "You are not needed on this side of the boards."

The woman did not make a move to obey at once, and Bob's eyes took on a threatening look.

"I mean what I say," he said, grimly; "I should hate to have to shoot a woman, but if you attack us I shall be forced to do so. We do not intend to allow ourselves to be captured, and our prisoner freed."

The woman decided, then, that it would be better to obey, and she turned and walked back to the fireplace.

The man followed suit, and the eager look which had appeared in the eyes of Captain Warwick died out, and a look of disappointment took its place.

He saw that the attempt that was to have been made to save him could not be made with any degree of safety. "Now you two people stay where you are until we give you permission to move!" said Dick, sternly, as he and Bob again took their seats and resumed eating.

The man and woman looked sullen, but made no reply. They had failed, and did not feel like talking.

When they had finished their meal, the youths again tied the hands of the prisoner.

"Now," said Dick, turning to the man, "bring our horses up to the door."

The youth spoke sternly.

He was not disposed to waste any politeness on a man who would have aided a British prisoner to escape.

This proved conclusively that the farmer was a Tory, and Dick liked Tories even less than he liked the redcoats.

The man made no reply in words, but rose and went out of doors.

Five minutes later the door reopened and he re-entered.

"Your hosses are ready," he said, shortly.

"Come," said Dick, and he took hold of Captain Warwick's arm.

Bob followed close behind Dick and the prisoner, and kept his eyes on the man and his wife.

He thought that they might try to attack Dick and himself and free the prisoner, even yet, if they got the chance, and he was determined they should not have the chance.

The horses stood in front of the door, and Dick and Bob helped the captain to mount.

Then Dick turned to the man, who had followed as far the door, where he stood watching them sullenly.

"Now, my Tory friend, how much do we owe you?" the youth asked, coolly; "we ought not by rights to pay you a cent, but we are willing to do so, just the same."

The man named a sum, which Dick paid, and then he and Bob mounted, and they rode away in the gathering darkness.

They had hardly more than disappeared from sight, when the man emerged from the house and set off across the field at a dog-trot.

He climbed another fence, and presently reached a log house standing in the edge of the timber.

He approached the house, and knocked on the door.

A moment later the door opened, revealing a tall, gaunt, rough-looking man in the garb of a hunter.

"Hello, Sykes!" the man cried; "come in."

The Tory farmer entered at once.

"What's the matter, Sykes? Ye look excited," the hunter said.

The farmer looked around the room before replying.

"Ah! the boys are here, I see," he said. "Good! Yes; I am excited," this last to the hunter; "I have good reason to be. Captain Warwick, who passed this way to-day, as you will remember, bearing important despatches to General Howe at New York, has just gone back in company with a couple of young rebels, who captured him. They are taking him to the rebel army, to turn him over to Washington."

"What!" exclaimed the hunter.

"What!" cried the other occupants of the room in chorus.

There were five others, making six men in all, besides Sykes, the farmer.

They were rough-looking men, all of them; men who seemed capable, if looks went for anything, of doing almost everything.

"Yes; Captain Warwick has been captured, an' is bein' took back a prisoner!" said Sykes. "They had supper at my house, an' hev jest started on their way. I've come over to git you fellows, an' ef we hurry we kin ketch 'em, an' git Captain Warwick outer them rebels' han's."

The men leaped to their feet.

"We're ready ter go with ye!" they cried in chorus.

"Come along, then!" cried Sykes.

"They're on horseback, hain't they?" asked the man in hunter garb.

"Yes; but we kin cut across through the timber, an' head 'em off at the bend, if we hurry."

"That's right; so we can."

The man left the house, and set out through the timber.

They walked rapidly, and it was evident that they knew every foot of the ground.

They kept up their swift gait for half an hour, and then they emerged into the road.

"I wonder if we got here in time?" remarked Sykes.

"I dunno." one of the others replied; "we'll know afore very long, though, I guess."

"Let's see if we can hear anything uv 'em," said Sykes.

Then he got down and placed his ear close to the frozen ground, while the others were silent.

He shook his head when he got up.

"Couldn't hear ennything," he said.

"They'll be along purty soon," said the hunter.

"You think we have got here ahead uv 'em, then?" Sykes asked.

"I think so; unless they rode faster than one would think for."

The men stood just within the edge of the timber, and waited patiently for perhaps five minutes, then the hunter got down and placed his ear close to the ground.

"They're coming!" he said, as he rose to his feet; "at enny rate, I hear the sound of hosses' hoofs on the ground."

The men cocked their rifles and stood in readiness, eagerly awaiting the appearance, at the bend fifty yards distant, of their expected victims.

CHAPTER IX.

THE YOUTHS OUTWIT THEIR FOES.

It was now rapidly getting dark.

It was just possible to see as far as the bend in the road, and before the party for which they were waiting reached the bend, it had become so dark it was possible to see only a few yards.

The men could hear the sound of the horses' feet, however, and knew the animals were close at hand.

They moved out and took their stand in the middle of the road.

Presently the horses loomed up in front of the six, and the leader cried:

"Halt! Stop, or you are dead men!"

The horses were brought to a stop at once, and an exclamation of fear and surprise was heard.

The six pressed forward, and then exclamations of surprise, rage and discomfiture escaped them.

There were three horses, all right, but there was only one person—a man—and he was mounted on the middle horse; on the backs of the other two horses were sacks vegetables, for the man was a farmer, en route to Trenton to sell his produce.

Curses escaped the lips of the disappointed men, and they asked the farmer if he had seen three men on horse back.

He replied that he had not.

"Then they must be ahead of us, after all," said Sykes; "come along, fellows; let's see if we can catch them!" The six ran up the road, leaving the farmer to follow at his leisure.

Sykes and his friends were dealing with no common youths when they thought to capture Dick and Bob.

The youths had not gone a hundred yards before Dick looked at Bob, and said:

"I didn't like the looks in the eyes of that fellow back there, old man; how was it with you?"

"The same; I'm of the opinion that he was figuring making us trouble in some way."

"That's what I think; now, what could he do?"

"He might have friends near, and they might try head us off."

"Just as like as not that is his scheme. Well, we must spoil his game, and there is only one way to do it."

"How, Dick?"

"By riding so rapidly that they could not possibly get through the timber and head us off."

"That's the best plan; if we go slow, they might be able to work it successfully."

"Yes; well, let's ride as fast as we can, Bob."

They urged their horses, and that of the British officer to a gallop, and rode forward at this rapid pace for more than half an hour.

The result was that they were a mile beyond the bend

in the road when the party under the leadership of Sykes reached the bend, and when the party stopped the farmer going to market, thinking he was the youths with their prisoner, the three were at least two miles away.

Of course, they had such a start that the party under Sykes, although they ran onward for a mile at least, did not lessen the distance between them.

The two youths made their way steadily onward, and they had approached as near to Trenton as they dared venture, and keep the road, and then they turned aside into the timber, and made their way toward the Delaware River.

The youths were beginning to be familiar with the lay of the land now, and they did not have much difficulty finding the cabin of Joe Saunders, the man who had taken them across the river two nights before.

Saunders was at home, and greeted the youths cordially. "So you have captured a redcoat and intercepted some important despatches, eh?" he remarked, when Dick had explained matters to him; "well, that is good. And, now, suppose you want me to put you across the river again?"

"That is just what we want, Joe," replied Dick; "will you do it?"

"Will I? Well, I just guess I will! You can count on old Joe to always be ready to do all he can to help the Cause! Do you want to go right ahead now, or shall I get you something to eat?"

"We have been to supper; we want to get across the river

as quickly as possible."

"Very well; come along, then."

Saunders led the way, and they were soon at the mouth of the creek.

The flatboat was there, and the youths led the horses onto it.

Then they assisted Captain Warwick to dismount, as in case the horses got to plunging while they were making the passage he might be thrown into the river.

Dick helped Saunders row, and twenty minutes later they were on the other shore.

Mounting their horses, they bade Saunders good-by, and rode away, the British officer between them.

They reached the encampment at last, and they went at once to the log house which was Washington's headquarters.

When the commander-in-chief saw that it was Dick and Bob with a prisoner, his eyes gleamed with pleasure.

"Who have you there, Dick?" he asked.

"Captain Warwick, of the king's troops, your excellency," replied Dick.

"Ah! Captain Warwick, be seated," said General Washinton, courteously, and the British officer dropped upon the couch, and looked about him with an air of ill-concealed disgust.

He eyed the commander-in-chief of the Continental army with eager gaze. Evidently he wished to see what manner of man it was who could, with so few men, cause well-drilled and equipped soldiers of the king so much trouble.

"Where did you capture the captain?" General Washington asked.

"About halfway between Trenton and Princeton, your excellency. He was on his way to New York with important despatches for General Howe."

Dick drew the papers from his pocket.

"Here they are," he said; "and here, also, is the communication from General Lee."

Dick handed the commander-in-chief the papers, and he took them; but before settling down to examine them he ordered that the prisoner be taken to the guard house.

This was done, and then, telling Dick and Bob to wait, he called General Greene, and they examined the papers that had been taken from the British officer.

The communication from General Lee was tossed aside to wait, as they had a good idea what its contents were without looking.

"Now, if Lee were only here with his troops, we might do something!" said General Greene, presently, when they had finished looking at the despatches that had been intended for the British commander-in-chief.

"True," said Washington, "but it seems as if General Lee and his army is fated to never reach us."

Then he took up the communication from General Lee, and opening it, read it through. His countenance gave no sign of what was passing in his mind as he read, and he passed the communication to General Greene with the remark:

"The usual story."

General Greene took the letter and read it, and returned it without comment.

The commander-in-chief took up the despatches to General Howe and went through them again.

"There is a lot of information of a general nature in these," he said.

"Yes, indeed," agreed Greene.

"You did a good thing when you captured Captain Warwick, my boys," the commander-in-chief said.

"We are very glad of that, your excellency," said Dick, modestly. "And if there is anything else that you wish us to do, we are ready to attempt it."

The commander-in-chief looked at General Greene, smiled, and then looked at Dick.

"There is only one thing that I know of that you could do, Dick," he said, "and that is to return to Lee with another 'hurry' order. That is the most important matter that claims our attention at present—the getting of Lee's army down here. With three thousand men we can do nothing, but with seven thousand we may, if the opportunity offers, do considerable. But it seems like asking too much to ask you to return to Lee's army again so soon."

"I only wish it were possible for us to appear before him, morning, noon and night, and in his dreams!" said Dick. "Perhaps he would move more rapidly then."

The youths were sure they saw a twinkle in the eyes of the commander-in-chief, so when he said with courteous graveness, "It is not seemly that a youth like you should critcise the actions of an officer of such rank as General Lee!" they did not feel so very bad.

"I crave your excellency's pardon!" said Dick, soberly.

"Granted, Dick," with a smile, and General Greene gave the youths a sly wink.

"Let me see," said the commander-in-chief, after a few minutes of silence; "this is the twelfth, is it not?"

"Yes, your excellency," replied Dick.

General Washington was silent for a while, and then he turned again to the youths.

"Are you willing to make another trip to Lee's army?" he asked.

"We are entirely at your service, your excellency," said Dick, promptly. "All we ask is four hours' sleep."

"You shall have it. Retire to that room there, and get to sleep at once. I will have you called when the time has expired."

The youths bowed, and then saluting, withdrew to the room indicated.

They threw themselves down on cots, and were soon asleep.

They were awakened by an orderly at two o'clock, and when they entered the main room there was the commander-in-chief, seemingly as wide awake as ever he had been in his life.

He gave the order that he had written to Lee, to Dick, and the youth placed it in his pocket.

"I hope I won't have to send you to General Lee many more times, my boys," he said with a smile.

"We are willing to make the trip as frequently as it may be necessary, your excellency," said Dick.

General Washington gave them a few more instructions, and then the youths saluted and withdrew.

They went and saddled and bridled their faithful horses, and ten minutes later they were riding away through the timber, headed for the Delaware River.

They went direct to the log house where the boat guard was located, and were soon on board a flat-boat and being taken across the river.

When they reached the other shore they bade the men who had brought them across good-by, and mounting their horses, rode away.

"We will learn this road pretty soon, eh, Dick?" laughed Bob, as they rode along.

"That's right, Bob; but say, did you ever see such a man as the commander-in-chief? Do you think he ever sleeps?"

"One would almost think that he never does, Dick," was the reply.

"He sits up into the small hours of the morning, thinking and thinking," said Dick, "while others are in bed sound asleep."

"I guess you are right, old man. Well, he is a wonderful

man; there is no doubt regarding that."

"Not a bit of doubt regarding it, Bob."

And every reader of history knows that the youths we right in their judgment of the commander-in-chief of the Continental Army.

They rode onward steadily, and when morning came they stopped at a farm house and ate breakfast.

Then they rode onward again steadily until near noon when they stopped at another farm house for dinner and feed for their horses.

After a rest of an hour they rode onward again, and they reached Morristown at half-past four o'clock.

When they arrived there they were surprised to find the patriot army there.

"This is a surprise, Bob," said Dick. "I never expected to find the army so far advanced as all this. General Lee must have made up his mind to hasten at last."

The youths ran across some of their acquaintances among the soldiers, and after exchanging a few words, asked where General Lee's headquarters were.

"Why, haven't you heard?" asked a soldier.

"Heard what?" asked Dick. "No, we haven't heard anything."

"What is it?"

"General Lee has been captured!"

"What!" exclaimed the youths in chorus. "Captured?"

"Yes; by the British this morning. He went down to Baskingridge, about four miles from here, and was surprised and captured by a party of dragoons."

"I'm glad of it!" declared Dick, with grim earnestness.

"And so am I!" said Bob. "I could shout 'Hurrah!'"

The soldiers grinned.

"We haven't any of us shed many tears!" he said.

"Who is in command here now?" inquired Dick.

"Sullivan," was the reply.

"He's all right," said Bob.

"Where will we find him?" asked Dick.

"In that tavern yonder," was the reply, and the soldier pointed to a tavern which stood down the street a ways.

"Come, Bob; we will report to him at once," said Dick and they rode to the tavern, and dismounting and tying their horses, entered the building.

"We have despatches for General Lee," said Dick to the orderly, "but as he has been captured, we will deliver them to General Sullivan. Show us to him at once."

"This way," said the orderly, and they were ushered into the presence of the acting commander.

"Ah, glad to see you, my boys!" said Sullivan, who knew the youths well. "Have you just arrived?"

"Yes," replied Dick, "with despatches for General Lee, which we will turn over to you as next in command," and Dick produced the order from the commander-in-chief to the officer.

CHAPTER X.

ENCOUNTERING AN OLD ENEMY.

General Sullivan took the despatch, and opening it, read the contents.

When he had finished he looked at Dick and asked:

"How soon will you be ready to return?"

"We could start back after a rest of three or four hours, sir," replied Dick.

"By ten o'clock, say?"

"Yes, sir."

"Very well; report here to me at ten o'clock. I will have an answer ready for you to take back to the commander-in-chief."

"Very well, sir."

Then the youths saluted and withdrew.

They first saw to it that their horses were taken care of, and then they hunted up their comrades whom they usually messed with, and from them they got the complete story the capture of General Lee.

He had gone to Baskingridge, four miles away, and had taken up his quarters in a tavern there; his presence had been discovered by a Tory, who had ridden in hot haste to the British encampment and had returned with thirty troopers, who had surrounded the tavern, and captured Lee, after which they rode back to the British encampment with their prisoner in triumph.

"And now," said the soldier who was telling the youths the story of the capture, "maybe we will reach General Washington and rejoin the rest of the army before spring, anyway."

Dick and Bob both said they hoped so.

"The commander-in-chief needs the men, I know that!" Dick.

When supper time came Dick and Bob ate with the soldiers, and they remained there talking and taking it easy until ten o'clock, and then they bade their friends good-by and made their way to the tavern and reported to General Sullivan.

He had the letter to the commander-in-chief written, and gave it to Dick, who put it in his pocket.

After some further instructions from the general, the youths saluted and withdrew.

They got their horses, mounted and rode away toward the south.

They rode steadily, with the exception of one resting period of half an hour, all the rest of the night, and reached Princeton early next morning.

They turned their horses over to the hostler of the tavern, where they intended to breakfast, and then entered the tavern.

The proprietor of the place eyed the youths searchingly.

"Traveled far?" he asked.

"Oh, so-so," was Dick's careless reply. He felt that it was no business of the landlord's how far they had traveled, yet he did not feel like telling him so.

"How soon will breakfast be ready?" asked Bob, who was hungry.

"Half an hour," was the reply.

The youths retired to the wash room and made their toilet, after which they re-entered the combined office and barroom, and took seats in front of the big fireplace.

"This is solid comfort, eh, Dick?" remarked Bob, with an air of satisfaction.

"Yes; this is all right, Bob."

"Rather more comfortable than riding in the cold night air, eh?" from the landlord, who had approached and was poking at the fire.

"Yes," said Dick, briefly.

Somehow he got it into his head that the landlord was trying to pump them.

"Did you say you came from the north?" the man remarked.

"I didn't say," replied Dick.

"Have you heard about the capture?" the landlord persisted.

He was certainly a hard man to discourage.

"What capture?" asked Bob.

"The capture of the American general, Lee. He was found in a tavern at Baskingridge this morning by a party of British dragoons, and was captured and taken to British headquarters."

"Oh, yes, we heard about that," said Dick, carelessly.

"They say it will end the war," the landlord continued. "It is said that Lee was the ablest general the Americans had, and now that he has been captured there is no one left who will be capable of keeping up the fight."

Dick and Bob looked at each other and laughed.

"I would like to know what the fellow Lee ever did to earn such a reputation," said Dick.

The landlord raised his eyebrows.

"You don't seem to think very highly of him," he said.

"I don't know of anything he has done that amounted to very much," replied Dick. "He has claimed credit that belonged to other men; that is all he has ever done."

"So, so! That is the way you look at it, eh?" the landlord exclaimed. "Do you, then, think Washington a greater general than Lee?"

"I certainly do think so," said Dick. "Lee isn't to be mentioned alongside of Washington. Washington is a great general, while Lee—well, the fact that he went off down by himself to an unguarded tavern is enough to prove that he was no general."

"Hum!" said the landlord. "Who are you gentlemen, that you know so much about Washington and Lee? You must be patriots, and pretty high up ones at that."

"That is nothing to you," said Dick, shortly. "Let us know when breakfast is ready, please."

The landlord grunted out something unintelligible, and stalked to the door and looked out.

"Ah," he said, "business is good this morning; here

comes a company of dragoons. I judge they are out hunting more American generals to capture."

Dick and Bob exchanged glances.

"Are they coming here, landlord?" asked Dick, calmly.

"Yes; they will be here in a few moments."

"Then let's get into the dining room at once, Bob," said Dick. "Remember, first come, first served, landlord. If they get into the dining room first, we would stand a poor chance of getting anything to eat."

Dick's scheme was to get out of the office and barroom before the redcoats entered. If he and Bob got seated at a table in the dining room they would be subjected to much less severe scrutiny than if they were to be in the barroom.

"Walk into the dining room and take a seat at one of the tables," said the landlord, suavely, and the youths obeyed.

They were careful to take their hats and overcoats with them, as they did not know but they might want to leave the dining room in a hurry, and possibly by a rear doorway.

They were careful to choose a table at the farther end of the room, and at the side, near a door.

They were equally careful to sit down upon the farther side of the table, so that they would be facing the redcoats when they should enter the room.

"Be prepared to act promptly, Bob," said Dick, in a low tone. "We are likely to get into trouble before we get away from here."

"I'll be ready to act when the time comes, Dick," was

the reply.

The youths, from where they sat at the table, could see the redcoats when they had entered, the connecting door being open.

They could hear what the troopers were talking about too, and soon learned that this was the very same patrol that had captured General Lee.

Encouraged by their success of the day before, they were out on a sort of scouting expedition, looking about, in the hope that they might make another important capture.

Suddenly Dick gave a start, and looking at Bob, said:

"We will have to get out of here at once, Bob! The commander of that crowd out there is Captain Frink, that old enemy of mine, whom I have twice wounded! He will recognize me the instant he lays eyes on me, and we will be taken prisoners in short order."

Dick rose as he spoke, and taking his overcoat under one arm, tip-toed to the door leading from the dining room the open air, Bob following.

Dick tried the knob, but it would not turn.

The door was locked!

Dick looked for the key, but it was not there.

A glance into the barroom showed the redcoats standing in front of the fireplace, laughing and talking.

They were warming themselves, but might come on into the dining room at any moment.

The situation of the two boy spies was desperate and dangerous in the extreme.

If the redcoats were to enter at once they would be caught like rats in a trap.

Dick looked about the room with eager, searching gaze.

At the same instant he heard the voice of Captain Frink say:

"Come on, my boys; let's go in and get something to eat and drink. I am both hungry and thirsty."

Dick's eyes fell upon a door at the opposite side of the room.

He realized that the door opened upon a stairway leading to the upper rooms of the tavern.

"Come, Bob, quick!" he said in a low tone, and he moved across the floor on his tip-toes, Bob keeping close behind him.

The door opened readily in response to Dick's touch, and they passed through and closed the door just as the redcoats began filing into the dining room.

The landlord came first, followed by Captain Frink, in turn being followed by the troopers.

When the landlord looked about the room and saw it was unoccupied he gave utterance to an exclamation of surprise.

"What's the matter?" asked Captain Frink.

"Why, where have they gone?" was all the landlord could say.

"Where have who gone?"

"The two young fellows."

"What two young fellows? We know nothing about

any young fellows."

"There were a couple of young men in here," the land-lord explained. "They entered just before you came into the tavern, and I don't see where they can have gone, or why, unless—"

He paused and looked at Captain Frink for a few moments, an eager light in his eyes.

"Unless what?" asked Captain Frink, in some impatience.

"Unless they were rebel spies, or something like that, and were afraid to meet you and your men!"

Captain Frink gave a start.

"Ah-ha!" he exclaimed. "It does look suspicious, their disappearing, doesn't it? What sort of looking fellows were they?"

"They were not much more than boys—about seventeen or eighteen years of age, I should say, and quite bright appearing and good looking."

Captain Frink gave another start.

For some reason the name and face of Dick Slater had appeared in his mind.

He could not account for it, but the thought came to him that the youths were the boy spies who had given General Howe and the British army so much trouble.

He had been well pleased when he had effected the capture, the morning before, of General Lee, but if the two youths in question should turn out to be Dick Slater and companion spy, Bob Estabrook, and he could capture them, Captain Frink would be much better pleased, and he doubted not that General Howe would learn of the capture with almost as great pleasure, for the youths had been as thorns in the British commander-in-chief's side. He had even offered rewards of one hundred pounds each for the capture of the youths.

Then, too, Captain Frink had a personal feeling in the matter. He and Dick had come in collision on two or three other occasions, and the youth had shot and wounded the worthy captain twice—once in the cheek, marring his beauty somewhat, and once in the arm, breaking that useful member.

Ah! Captain Frink would have given much to capture Slater, the boy spy!

Dick was well aware of this fact, and was not disposed to let Captain Frink do this.

Captain Frink looked eagerly around the room.

"Where can they have gone?" he asked. "Out of doors?" pointing to the door leading to the open air.

The landlord shook his head.

"That door is locked," he said.

Frink's eyes lighted upon the door leading to the stairway.

"Where does that lead to?" he asked, eagerly.

The landlord gave a start.

"Upstairs. Do you think—"

"I think nothing, but we have got to find out! I have a consuming curiosity to lay eyes on those youths you have spoken of; I fancy I shall know them when I see them! Lead the way upstairs, landlord, and at once. We must not give the young rascals much time, or they will escape us. If they are who I think they are, they are as slippery as eels."

The men were looking interested and excited now.

They scented more glory ahead in the capture of some more rebels.

The landlord led the way across the room, and taking hold of the knob of the door leading to the stairway, turned it, and pulled the door open.

There was no one in sight.

"They have gone on upstairs!" cried Captain Frink. "Lead the way, landlord!"

The landlord obeyed, and led the way up the stairs, the captain keeping close at his heels, and the men trooping along after the captain.

The captain drew his sword, and his men drew their dragoon pistols.

"They cannot escape us!" cried Captain Frink, in a loud voice. "We have them cornered, and will capture them easily."

The captain spoke loudly purposely, so that the fugitives might hear him. He thought it might serve to break their nerve somewhat.

Which showed that he did not yet know what sort of a youth Dick Slater was.

CHAPTER XI.

THE ESCAPE.

DICK and Bob had hastened on up the stairs and along a hall which extended back toward the rear of the building, as well as forward toward the front.

"Let's go to the rear," said Dick. "The stable is in that direction, and we will have to go to the stable to get our horses. I won't leave without Major, if I have to fight Captain Frink and his entire gang."

"Lead on; I'll follow," said Bob, grimly.

They hastened back along the hall until they reached its end.

There was no window in the end of the building looking out from the hall, and Dick opened a door at the left hand and entered a room.

It was a corner room, and had two windows.

Dick hastened to the side window and looked out.

"No shed or anything there to break our fall if we should jump out," he said.

Then he passed on to the window in the end of the room.

"This is all right, Bob," he said; "there's a roof of a shed or something a couple of feet below the window. We can get out here all right."

At this instant the loud voice of Captain Frink was heard, and the youths understood his words.

"So you think you have us cornered, and that we cannot escape, eh, Captain Frink?" murmured Dick, grimly. "Well, we'll show you whether you have or not!"

Then Dick seized hold of the window and raised it.

"Get through, quick, Bob!" Dick said in a low tone. "We will have to hurry!"

Bob obeyed without a word.

He climbed through the window quickly, and then Dick followed, letting the window slide back down into its place as he did so.

The youths found themselves standing on a slanting roof.

It was not so steep but what they could keep their feet by being careful, and they made their way down to the edge, where the distance was only about ten feet to the ground, and leaped down.

"Come!" said Dick, and they hastened toward the stable. Just as they reached the stable door they heard a great shout, and, looking back, saw the faces of the landlord and Captain Frink at the window through which they had just escaped.

"There they are!" howled the worthy captain. "There they are! Hurry, men; jump through this window here and capture them! They are the rebel spies, Dick Slater and Bob Estabrook! On your lives, don't let them escape!"

The captain did not wish to risk climbing out on the sloping roof in his stiff riding boots, but he was quite willing his men should risk breaking their necks.

Dick and Bob leaped through the doorway into the stable, and seizing the bridles, quickly bridled their horses. The saddles had not been removed.

Then they hastily led the horses out of the stable, just as a half dozen of the troopers came sliding down the sloping roof and half fell, half leaped to the ground.

The youths leaped into the saddles, and as the redcoats came running forward to meet them they urged their horses into a gallop.

Captain Frink, from the open window, shrieked commands to his men, and drawing a pistol, fired at Dick, the bullet whistling past the youth's ear.

"Try again, Captain Frink!" cried Dick, and then he drew a pistol, as did Bob also, and as their horses plunged into the crowd of redcoats the youths both fired in the fellows' faces.

They rode through and over the redcoats in a twinkling and then with defiant yells they rode past the tavern, and turning up the street, raced away at a gallop.

They looked back, and saw the redcoats running to their horses and mounting in hot haste.

"They're going to give chase, Bob," said Dick, with a grim smile.

"Let 'em!" grinned Bob. "They'll have to have a whole lot better horses than I think they have if they catch us."

"You are right, old man," smiled Dick, and then he leaned forward and patted Major on the neck.

Dick had had many a hard race with the redcoats when

mounted on the back of the horse he was riding, and never yet had he been outrun. Major had always shown the pursuers a clean pair of heels, and Dick was sure he could do so again.

Bob's horse was only a little less speedy, and the youth felt confident that they would be able to get away from the pursuing redcoats.

The redcoats came racing after them, however, and that they had been strenuously urged to overtake the fugitives was evident in the manner in which they belabored the poor beasts which they bestrode.

"Captain Frink would give considerable to be able to take us prisoners," said Dick, after a glance behind.

"Yes; he has it in for you, Dick. He will never be satisfied until after he has got even with you for wounding him those two times."

"Right, Bob; but he'll have to wait a while longer. I don't think I can let him square the account this morning."

Dick and Bob slowly but steadily drew away from the pursuers, and it was evident that it was, barring accident, only a question of time when the redcoats would be distanced.

They hung on, however, with great persistency.

They seemed determined to not give up.

They could not help seeing that their horses were not equal to those of Dick and Bob in speed, but they doubtless hoped that the horses of the fugitives might give out, and they would then be able to capture their riders.

It was a vain hope, but of course they did not know it.

They kept up the pursuit energetically.

Onward raced pursuers and pursued.

Past farmhouses the horsemen dashed, and the Jersey farmers rubbed their eyes and stared at the spectacle.

The affair was easy enough to understand.

The redcoated men were British; the two youths in ordinary clothing were patriots.

One farmer would yell encouragingly to the youths, and maintain a sullen silence as the redcoats rode by; while another would jeer the youths and cheer their pursuers.

But Dick and Bob did not worry.

They felt confidence in their ability to escape, and could afford to laugh at the Tories.

Onward rushed pursuers and pursued, and slowly but steadily Dick and Bob drew away, until after an hour of hard riding they found themselves a good mile in the lead, and following a winding road through the timber.

They rounded a bend in the road, and then they slackened the speed of the horses.

"Here is the place where we turn into the timber, Bob," said Dick, and leaving the road, they entered the woods.

"I guess this will fool those redcoats a bit," chuckled Bob. "They will go rushing on past, and will wonder where we went."

They rode onward, and presently came to the cabin of Joe Saunders.

Joe was at home, and took them across the Delaware

River without delay.

"What's the news, boys?" he asked.

"General Lee has been captured by the British," replied Dick.

Saunders evidently knew something regarding Lee, for he did not seem dismayed by the news.

"I guess it might have been worse," he said quietly.

As soon as they got ashore, on the opposite side of the River, the youths mounted and rode away toward the encampment of the patriot army.

They arrived there twenty minutes later, and went at once to the headquarters of the commander-in-chief. General Washington was not expecting them so soon, and was surprised, and seemed delighted to see them.

"What, back so soon?" he exclaimed. "How happens this?"

"We had not so far to go, your excellency; the army was in Morristown," said Dick.

"Say you so? That is indeed good news. And you saw General Lee?"

"No," said Dick. "General Lee was captured yesterday morning by the British, and we reported to General Sullivan as the next in command."

"What is that? Lee captured?" cried the commander-in-chief.

"Yes, your excellency, and here is a letter from General Sullivan which will, I judge, explain everything."

The commander-in-chief took the letter and read it

through, and then he called General Greene and told him the news.

"Wasn't that a foolish thing to do, his going away off down to that tavern by himself?" exclaimed General Washington, referring to Lee.

"It certainly was, your excellency," said Greene, "and he paid dearly for it."

"There is one thing that gives me pleasure, at any rate," said the commander-in-chief; "that is the fact that General Schuyler has sent seven regiments down from Lake Champlain. Sullivan says that he will hasten on down to join us just as soon as Gates and the troops reach him at Morristown. When they get here we will have enough men to enable us to strike the enemy a hard blow."

"True, your excellency," agreed General Greene.

The commander-in-chief did not seem greatly cast down over the capture of General Lee, and indeed there was no reason why he should be, for Lee had given him more trouble the past month or so than the entire British army.

Ten days later Sullivan and Gates, with three thousand men, joined Washington and his army across the Delaware, in Pennsylvania, and the commander-in-chief began figuring on dealing the enemy a blow that would show them plainly that the great cause of liberty was not dead, or even sleeping.

THE END.

LANDMARKS YOU CAN VISIT TODAY

1. Ford Mansion at Morristown National Historical Park
    > There's an excellent Revolutionary War museum and nearby monuments and buildings
2. Historical Marker at the corner of Colonial Drive and S. Finley Avenue in Bernards, New Jersey
    > Site of White's Tavern, where American General Charles Lee was captured by the British
3. Marker at 50 College Avenue in New Brunswick
    > A map highlights many places important to the war around the Rutgers University campus
4. John Hart's Cave historical marker, corner of Zion and Lindbergh Roads, in Hopewell, New Jersey
    > A signer of the Declaration of Independence, Hart fled Trenton after the British invaded and took refuge in this cave
5. British Occupation of New Jersey Marker
    > At Princeton Battlefield State Park
6. Summerseat House in Pennsylvania
    > George Washington's headquarters was here after he crossed the Delaware River

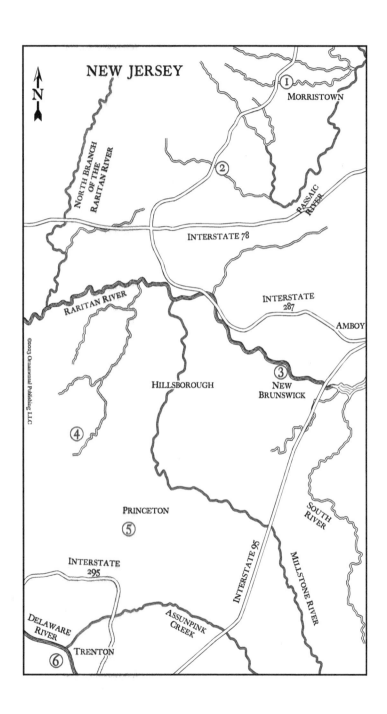

THE LIBERTY BOYS OF '76.

Follow the adventures of Captain Dick Slater and his band of brave Liberty Boys as they battle the British Empire for American independence!

WITH MORE TO COME!

Want more Liberty Boys?

www.thelibertyboysof76.com

ORNAMENTAL
PUBLISHING LLC